W9-ANP-370

1
SUSAN SAND
MYSTERY STORIES
THE MYSTERY AT
HOLLOWHEARTH HOUSE

# THE MYSTERY AT HOLLOWHEARTH HOUSE

MARILYN EZZELL

PINNACLE BOOKS NEW YORK

This is a work of fiction. All the characters and events portrayed in this book are fictional, and any resemblance to real people or incidents is purely coincidental.

SUSAN SAND MYSTERY #1: THE MYSTERY AT HOLLOWHEARTH HOUSE



An original Pinnacle Books edition, published for the first time anywhere.

First printing, August 1982

ISBN: 0-523-41701-2

**Cover illustration and illustrations in text by Hector Garrido**

*Printed in the United States of America*

PINNACLE BOOKS, INC.
1430 Broadway
New York, New York 10018

To my mother
with love and appreciation
and
in memory of my father

## *Contents*

## Chapter I

## *An Award and an Inheritance*

SUSAN SAND, a striking-looking girl with long black hair, dressed in green, and wearing pert eyeglasses, stood on the platform of the large auditorium and with a modest smile acknowledged the audience's thunderous applause. A tall, smiling man in a gray business suit stepped rapidly forward, warmly shook her hand, and presented her with an elegant bronze statuette.

"Miss Sand," he said in a loud, clear voice, "as president of Mystery Authors of America, I take great pleasure in presenting to you our award for your outstanding mystery novel, *The Bony Finger*. And might I add that, at nineteen, you are the youngest author ever to receive this honor."

Again the audience broke into loud applause as the girl graciously accepted the statuette and stepped to the lectern.

"I can't begin to tell you how very happy you have all made me by presenting to me this coveted award," she began, her voice quiet and lilting. "I wish to thank my aunt, Professor Adele Sand, for her astute criticism, Professor Randall Scott for his help on historical data, and my good friend Marge Halloran for her invaluable advice. I could not possibly name all the other people who encouraged me, so I will thank you en masse and say again how very happy you have made me."

The applause was again deafening as Susan took a little bow and resumed her seat. Scanning the sea of faces below her, she finally came to the freckled face of Marge Halloran, her best friend. Marge, who hadn't an ounce of jealousy in her, seemed to be applauding more vigorously than anyone else. Susan flashed her a fond smile.

Standing in the back of the crowded room was another close friend, the handsome Randall Scott. Susan smiled warmly at him, for he was actually waving to her in his boyish enthusiasm.

When the awards and the speeches were over, refreshments were served in the lounge. Because Susan Sand was the main celebrity, the young author was constantly asked to autograph copies of her book, while flashbulbs burst from all sides as newspaper photographers repeatedly snapped her picture. The festivities did not end until long after midnight, and only then could Susan and her aunt say goodnight to the well-wishers and return to their home.

Once they were inside the lovely big house, Professor Sand placed the statuette on the mantelpiece. Then, turning to her niece, she affectionately embraced her. "I am very proud of you, Susan," she said. "*The Bony Finger* is a fine achievement. There is no mystery story writer who is more deserving of this award than you."

"I can't believe the critics presented it to me," Susan replied, her green eyes sparkling with elation. "I'm so excited I won't be able to sleep for a week!"

However, after tumbling wearily into bed, the exhausted girl fell immediately into a peaceful slumber and did not awaken until early the next morning, when the telephone at her bedside rang loudly.

"Sue, it's me," came the excited voice of Marge Halloran over the wire. "I'm sorry to call so early, especially after last evening, but I've just received the most astounding telegram. I must see you right away."

"What on earth is the matter?" asked Susan, now fully awake. "Where are you calling from?"

"I'm just leaving for the bookstore. Can you go there right away and meet me?"

"Of course," replied Susan. "I'm on my way."

"Who was that on the phone, Sue?" called Susan's aunt from downstairs.

"Marge," replied Susan. "She has some important news."

"You'll have to tell me about it later," came Professor Sand's reply. "I have an appointment with one of my students at the university. I'll see you this afternoon."

Susan heard the front door close as she hurried into her clothes. After a quick breakfast, prepared by their housekeeper, Mrs. Draper, she kissed her cat, Icky, and rushed out to her green sports car, which was parked in the driveway. On the road to the main street of Thornewood, where Marge Halloran ran a bookstore with her mother, Susan passed the imposing campus of Irongate University.

The young author's entire life was intimately connected with that prestigious center of education, because her parents had taught there many years before. They had both been killed in a tragic accident when Susan was only five years old, and since that time her father's sister, Adele Sand, had been the girl's guardian. The name of Sand, already well known in Thornewood, had taken on a new luster with the success of Susan's first book. Aunt Adele, who was a professor of art history at Irongate, had always maintained that Susan would be the most famous member of the family.

A light rain had started to fall when Susan parked her car and hurried along the street to the small bookstore in the center of town. A little thrill went through her as she saw her own book displayed prominently in the window.

"How nice of Marge Halloran to give me such advertising," thought Susan Sand. "You'd think *The Bony Finger* was the only book in her store!"

No sooner had Susan entered the shop, the door closing slowly behind her, than a man stepped from behind a nearby telephone booth and thrust his foot into the opening to keep the door from shutting. Susan, completely unaware of the figure behind her, had already crossed the small book-lined store to an entrance leading to the back room.

"Marge, it's me," called Susan. "I came as soon as I could. I can hardly wait to hear your news."

"Come on in here, Sue," answered an excited voice. "I'm making coffee."

The bell over the street door jangled shrilly as the door closed, but not before the mysterious man had slipped unseen into the store and hidden behind a table of books.

"I can't thank you enough for displaying my book in such a prominent place," said Susan warmly. "Why, it's just bound to sell well with you on my side!"

"It's a good book, and I've already had to order more copies," replied Marge with a professional air. "Did you know your picture is on the front page of the *Thornewood Times*?"

Marge was a pretty, plump redheaded girl, engaged at the moment in making coffee on a hotplate. Susan looked at her fondly.

"Is it really—so soon?" she asked. "But let's stop talking about me. Why this early summons, Marge? I'm so full of curiosity, I can't wait another minute to hear the news."

"It's Hollowhearth House, Sue," replied Marge Halloran. "I've inherited it! It's all mine now!"

"Inherited Hollowhearth! That big old place out on Hollowhearth Hill? That's a wonderful piece of news!" replied Susan, hugging her friend. "But how on earth did it come about? I thought Bruce Webb was the owner."

Susan adjusted her glasses and studied Marge with keen, intelligent eyes. Marge Halloran was Susan Sand's oldest and dearest friend. Although they were both just nineteen, their friendship was of many years' duration, and the two girls were almost like sisters.

"Bruce Webb did own Hollowhearth, Sue," replied Marge, her expression suddenly becoming more serious. "But now he's dead, and even though he was a crook and stole the house from my grandfather, he left it to me in his will. He must have felt guilty. I suppose I should feel bad about the accident."

"Dead! What accident? Marge, what are you talking about? What happened to Bruce Webb?"

"He was coming back from Caracas, Venezuela, by ship, when a terrible storm came up and the ship sank. You must have heard about it on the radio. No one survived."

"Yes, I did hear about it within the last week. There was a report on television several days ago. But how do you know Bruce Webb was one of the passengers?"

"Mother and I received a telegram early this morning from the steamship company," replied Marge, pouring out Susan's coffee and placing the mug on a little table. "Apparently before he sailed from Caracas, in response to questions asked of passengers, he had listed Hollowhearth House as his address and mother and me as his next of kin. He didn't have any other family, and he was a distant relative of my grandfather's."

As Susan Sand listened intently to her friend's tale, there was a slight movement in the mirror on the wall opposite the door. Momentarily Susan was stunned, for she saw a hand, large and squat, gripping the doorframe. Someone was eavesdropping on their conversation! Susan could not see the person's body, for it was flattened against the wall, but the hand was obviously a man's. The knuckles were white as they gripped the wood, and completely motionless, as if frozen onto the doorframe.

Susan Sand was a cool and clear-headed girl. Aware that Marge and she could be in grave danger, she tried to keep her voice normal and not betray the fact that she had discovered the man's presence. Marge had not seen the hand, for she was facing away from the mirror, and the door itself hid the hand from her view.

"You know, Marge, I hadn't realized it was so late," said Susan, calmly looking at her watch. "I have an important appointment with my publisher in New York City, and if I'm going to get there on time, I'd better get going."

Susan started to edge slowly toward the door, making as little noise as possible. The hand remained motionless. Susan did not want to frighten Marge, for a sudden exclamation from her might warn the intruder, and Susan was determined to discover his identity.

"You're leaving! But it's not even eight-thirty. I haven't told you all the news yet," protested Marge, puzzled at the sudden change in Susan's attitude.

"I'll come back as soon as I can," replied Susan, edging nearer the door. The hand did not move, and as Susan crept closer she noticed a tattoo on the man's wrist, which depicted a small black bird perched on a gold circlet.

While Susan's eyes were riveted on the strange mark, the hand suddenly disappeared, and footsteps could be heard running across the store. Instantly Susan Sand was through the door and was racing after the man, just in time to see a hunched-over figure in a trenchcoat and rain hat jerk open the street door and plunge into the rain.

"Stop!" cried Susan as she ran after the man, unmindful of any possible danger. But already he had entered a battered old blue car and was turning the corner before Susan reached the curb.

"What is it, Susan?" gasped Marge as she reached her friend's side. "Who was that?"

"I don't know," replied Susan. "He must have crept into the store and been hiding when I arrived, or perhaps he slipped in after me."

As the two girls watched the car disappear, Susan quickly explained to Marge that she had seen the stranger's hand in the mirror. "By the time I reach my car he will be too far away for me to catch up with him. I had to park two blocks from here," she said ruefully. "Let's go back to the store, Marge. There's nothing we can do."

"Maybe we should call the police," said Marge. "He may have been a thief." Quickly she checked the cash register, but there was no money missing.

"If he were a thief he would have robbed the cash register and escaped without being seen," replied Susan.

She fingered her eyeglasses thoughtfully, and her emerald-green eyes shone with excitement.

"He was listening to our conversation," she mused half to herself. "He was so anxious to hear what we were saying that he risked discovery. There's only one explanation, Marge. He was trying to learn something about Hollowhearth House."

"But why, Sue?" said Marge, her voice quivering

ooks

and her face pale. "What interest could an absolute stranger possibly have in Hollowhearth House?"

"I can't answer that question right now," replied Susan, her eyes narrowing. "But there must be a secret connected with that old place, and I'm going to discover what it is."

## Chapter II

## *A Puzzling Find*

"OOH, I'm frightened," said Marge Halloran, sinking onto a stool. "I thought inheriting Hollowhearth House was going to be fun, but now I don't know what to think."

"You mustn't let this upset you, Marge," replied Susan gently but firmly. "I want you to tell me all you know about Hollowhearth House. There has to be a connection between that intruder and your inheritance, or he wouldn't have crept in here to eavesdrop on our conversation."

"Well, to begin with, you know how valuable the house is, Sue," replied Marge, brushing her red hair away from her face. "You've seen it from the cliff road high up on Hollowhearth Hill. The Hollow family built the house in 1830 and gave it the name of Hollowhearth. They lived there for almost a century, until my grandfather bought the property from young Kenneth Hollow."

"Didn't Bruce Webb swindle your grandfather out of the property?" asked Susan.

"Yes, Sue, he did. You could actually say Bruce Webb stole the whole place. He forced grandfather to sign the house over to him, supposedly in payment of a debt. My grandfather was old at the time and didn't fully realize what he was doing. Our family always knew that he had been tricked and that the debt had already been paid, but once the deed was in Bruce Webb's name, nothing could be done about the transaction. Grandfather died several months later."

"How cruel!" exclaimed Susan hotly. "I remember your grandfather well. Imagine cheating an old man out of his home. I thought at the time that any decent person would have been ashamed to move in. Did Bruce Webb live there long? I thought the place had been empty for years."

"Five years, to be exact. Bruce Webb disappeared five years ago, right after he took possession of the house," explained Marge. "No one knew where he had gone."

"And suddenly he turns up on a ship bound for New York from Venezuela. How strange." Susan sat quietly thoughtful for several moments. "I wonder what he was doing in South America and why he decided to return."

"Well, we'll never know, now that Bruce Webb is dead," returned Marge.

"I think we should try to forget about him and concentrate on Hollowhearth House," said Susan with spirit.

"You're right, Sue," replied Marge enthusiastically.

"I've been doing a lot of thinking since this morning. Wouldn't it be great to restore the house to its original condition?"

"What a wonderful idea!"

"The rooms are full of all sorts of old weapons, furniture, clothes, uniforms, medals. . . . Of course, a lot of money would be needed."

"You'd have an important museum!" exclaimed Susan. "Maybe the Thornewood Historical Society would be interested."

"Oh, that would be wonderful. You know so many interesting people, Sue. Professor Scott at Irongate, for example—the handsome Randall Scott," added Marge, casting a sly smile at her attractive friend. "He might be willing to offer his advice on how to go about such a project."

"Yes, Professor Scott may be the very person we need," replied Susan, pretending not to have noticed Marge's teasing glance. "I think he would be happy to help us."

"Oh, I hope so. Why not call him right now?" asked Marge impetuously.

"I'll dial his secretary this minute," said Susan, jumping up and going to the telephone.

In less than three minutes she was back, smiling triumphantly.

"We can see him tomorrow morning, Marge," she said. "I made an appointment for eleven-thirty."

"What luck!" cried her friend. "I'm glad to have such a busy day ahead of me. That way the time will pass more quickly."

* * *

The next morning the two girls drove the short distance to the university and entered the campus through the impressive old black iron gates, which were flanked by gray stone pillars. The tallest structure on the spacious grounds, visible from many parts of the town of Thornewood, was the university's chapel, whose white wooden spire rose majestically into the sky. A large clock in the stone tower of another building chimed out the quarter-hour as the car moved slowly down College Walk between huge poplar trees.

The number of students hurrying along the winding gravel paths indicated that classes were changing. Susan parked the car near the oldest building on campus, Piper Hall, in front of which stood a statue. The figure was that of Sebastian Iron, the great educator who had founded Irongate College in 1796.

Marge burst into giggles at the sight of a football helmet, which some student must have placed on the imposing statue's head, and Susan said, laughing, "The last time I was here he had a bright red mustache done with nail polish."

"I'd better stop giggling and try to compose myself," said Marge. "What is Professor Scott like, Sue? I'm a little reluctant to meet him. After all, we have come to ask a favor."

"Oh, he's very nice. You'll see," replied the slender, black-haired girl, hurrying her friend toward the entrance of Piper Hall.

The building was nearly empty, except for several impressive-looking men whom Marge judged to be professors. Several of them smiled and nodded to Susan, who in turn whispered to Marge who each one was.

"You know so many interesting people, Sue. Some of these professors come into the bookstore, but they never seem to remember me," said Marge, somewhat awed by the recognition her friend received.

Professor Scott's office was on the second floor, and the girls had to climb a flight of stairs in the old stone house, which had obviously once been a private home. As they paused on the landing, where the steps took a sharp turn, Susan noticed a small stained-glass window through which the sun was shining.

"What does that emblem remind me of?" she said, stopping to examine it as Marge, in her impatience, tried to pull her on.

"It's only the American eagle, Sue, for heaven's sake," said Marge. "But it's a horrible-looking one."

"It's absolutely menacing, but it isn't an eagle," said Susan as her friend urged her up the stairs.

Stopping before a glass door which bore the legend *PROFESSOR RANDALL SCOTT, CHAIRMAN, HISTORY DEPARTMENT,* Susan knocked and walked in. A pleasant secretary seated behind a huge desk confirmed their appointment and asked them to sit down. Disappearing momentarily into an inner office, she soon reappeared and told the girls that Professor Scott would see them right away. Susan rose and started for the door, but Marge did not budge.

"I think I'll stay here," she explained shamefacedly. "You can talk better than I can."

"Marge Halloran, you are coming right in here with

me," ordered Susan, grasping her hand. "Professor Scott is as nice a man as you could meet."

"I'm glad to hear you feel that way, Sue," said a masculine voice.

In the doorway to the inner office stood a husky man, extremely young in appearance, who looked far more like a football player than like a scholarly professor. He was smiling broadly, his hands on his hips and a mischievous twinkle in his brown eyes.

"It's nice to see you again," he continued, crossing the room and extending his hand to Susan, who was somewhat flushed at having her words of praise overheard.

After she had introduced him to Marge, the girls entered the inner office and sat down in large leather chairs.

"He's so young," whispered Marge, unable to conceal her admiration, "and very attractive."

The professor, still smiling, was regarding Susan warmly. "Thanks for mentioning me in that acceptance speech the other night, Sue. I didn't deserve it for the little bit of historical data I supplied for your book."

"I'll probably be asking you to check some of the facts for my next book," said Susan, adjusting her glasses. "But we didn't come to discuss my books. We came to ask your advice."

As Randall Scott settled back in his chair, Susan began to relate the story of Marge's inheritance of Hollowhearth House. The young man's interest was evident from the first, for he rested his chin on one hand and listened carefully to every word.

"So you see," concluded Susan, "Marge feels that a lot can be done with the house. Now that the property is hers, she is free to do whatever she wants."

"You say that Bruce Webb owned the house?" asked Randall Scott.

"That's right," replied Marge. "Although he cheated grandfather to get it, he did leave it to me in his will. Evidently he had a guilty conscience. He must have known my grandfather intended to leave the house to me."

Professor Scott's smile faded, and a frown appeared on his face.

"You may be interested to know that I was a classmate of Bruce Webb. In fact, we were very friendly in college."

"What!" cried the girls simultaneously, for they could not imagine the two men having anything in common.

"Perhaps I felt sorry for him because he didn't have many friends. He was difficult to get along with and never considered honesty an important attribute. During our third year in college he was expelled for stealing an automobile."

"Did you see him much after that?" asked Marge.

Randall Scott rose to his feet and began pacing back and forth behind his desk, his hands clasped behind him.

"We corresponded for a while, but never saw each other again. Not once in any of his letters did he mention Hollowhearth House. I can certainly understand why. I had always hoped that he would straighten out. I knew he had gone to Venezuela, but he wrote to me only once from there and mentioned that he was going to be married. At any rate, he stopped communicating with me quite a while ago."

Professor Scott stopped pacing the floor and turned to address Marge. "I think your idea of restoring Hollowhearth House is a very worthwhile one," he said, thrusting his hands in his pockets. "Of course, I will have to see the place before I can say definitely—that is, if you want me to visit it."

"Oh, that would be wonderful!" cried Marge, forgetting her former shyness. "When can you come with us?"

Susan caught a slight wink as Randall Scott thoughtfully wrinkled his brow. "If we eat lunch now, we can reach Hollowhearth by two o'clock," he said, glancing at his watch.

"But first Marge and I have something else to tell you—something that happened yesterday morning," interjected Susan. "Apparently the three of us are not the only people interested in that old place."

Marge remained silent and looked a little pale beneath her freckles as Susan told Professor Scott about the stealthy intruder who had hidden in the bookstore, eavesdropping on their conversation about Hollowhearth House.

"Before he fled," continued Susan, "I got a very good look at a tattoo on his wrist. It was a black bird, sort of like a raven, perched on what looked like a golden circle with points."

Randall Scott let out a low, soft whistle and was about to speak when Susan, springing from her chair, exclaimed, "Now I remember! That's what's on the window!"

Without pausing to explain, she ran from the room and down the stairs to the landing, with Marge and Randall Scott close on her heels.

"That," said Susan, pointing to the small stained-glass window, "is exactly what I saw tattooed on that man's wrist!"

"But that's not logical, Susan," said Professor Scott as he gazed intently at the little panes of colored glass. "What possible connection could there be between your mysterious intruder and this window?"

"I know it sounds implausible," replied Susan with feeling, "but there is absolutely no doubt in my mind that the two emblems are identical."

The three of them stood dumbfounded.

"A black bird," said Susan almost in a whisper. "Whatever could it mean?"

## Chapter III

## *A Shock*

SUSAN SAND and her two companions remained standing on the landing of the stairway, studying the window, each of them straining to think of some reasonable connection between it and the tattoo on the wrist of the mysterious interloper.

"That is obviously some family's coat of arms," said Professor Scott, bending down to scrutinize further the stained-glass escutcheon. "A fierce-looking black bird perched on a golden crown on a green background," he mused.

Straightening to his full height, he turned toward Susan and Marge and continued, "I have wondered ever since I started to teach here who installed this window and when. This house changed owners many times before Irongate College purchased it way back in 1796 from the Piper family. I have done plenty of research on its history, but nowhere have I come across the faintest clue to this."

He tapped the glass with his forefinger. "Your story, Susan, is positively eerie."

"It gives me the creeps," said Marge with a shiver, glancing over her shoulder as though expecting to see someone behind her.

"I think we should discuss this during lunch," said Randall Scott, and then he took each girl by the arm and escorted them down the stairs.

The trio left the old building and crossed the campus to the university dining room. With this new discovery, Susan was convinced that she must unearth the identity of the hunched-over man in the trench-coat, but her brief glimpse of him had left the young sleuth with very few clues. A connection between the man's tattoo and the window seemed preposterous, but Susan had no doubt that in some strange way the two were related.

Once in the dining room, they were shown to a table, and while Susan scanned the menu she could not help noticing Marge's elation over lunching in this picturesque hall with an important professor. Susan had been here many times with Randall Scott, and she was happy now to be able to share this pleasure with her friend.

They had no sooner started to eat than a gray-haired little man with a goatee, very scholarly in appearance and carrying a briefcase, entered the dining room. Momentarily glancing about, he espied Professor Scott and started to hurry over to the table where the trio was seated.

"That's Dr. Giles Endicott," whispered Randall Scott. "He's an eminent archeologist and he also teaches in the History Department. He's leaving for

South America tonight to do some research. I'll be teaching some of his classes while he's away."

"I've heard of him before," replied Susan admiringly. "He's been all over the world and he's written many books of value. I'm glad to get the chance to meet him."

After being introduced to Marge and Susan, Dr. Endicott sat down for a few moments to chat. He was an amusing, likable man who talked in short, clipped sentences and cast quick glances from one person to another as he spoke.

"I have been wanting to meet the author of *The Bony Finger*," he said, leaning close to Susan as though to share a delightful secret. "An astonishing piece of work, Miss Sand, astonishing."

"It gives me great pleasure to have you say that," said Susan, trying hard not to reveal how elated she was to receive such an appraisal of her book from a person of Professor Endicott's standing.

"And did a mystery bring you to Irongate today?" he asked in a mischievous tone.

"Perhaps," Susan replied enigmatically, and quickly she told him about Marge's inheritance of Hollowhearth House and about the strange happenings that all three of them felt must be connected with it.

Dr. Endicott listened attentively and knitted his brows into a deep furrow. "If you keep on writing mysteries until you're ninety-nine years old, Miss Sand, you will never top this one," he said.

He had become very serious. "My, oh, my," he breathed, pulling his goatee and letting his gaze wander to some faraway place where, his companions felt, his fine brain was grappling with the strange mystery connected with Hollowhearth House.

Then, glancing at his watch, the little man sprang to his feet and explained that he had a great deal to do before his departure for South America. Digging into his briefcase, he pulled out several papers and handed them to Professor Scott.

"These are some of my lectures which I thought you might find helpful," he remarked.

And to Susan he said, "Work on it, but be careful, Miss Sand. I don't like the sound of this; there could be danger, grave danger."

Bidding the trio farewell, he hurried from the room.

"What a delightful man," said Susan thoughtfully. "I think he's as interested in this mystery as we are."

"Knowing Dr. Endicott, I'm sure he is," returned Randall Scott. "But we had better hurry too. It's nearly one-thirty, and we want to get a good look at Hollowhearth House before dusk."

The main highway took them toward their destination, but the last few miles had to be traveled on the narrow, winding cliff road that climbed up Hollowhearth Hill. Since it was not paved, it was almost impassable. Years must have gone by since the grounds had been tended, for the private road was nearly swallowed up by thick underbrush and was strewn with large stones.

A quarter of a mile beyond, set on the high part of the hill, stood Hollowhearth House. At one time a beautiful home, the old gray stone house was now eerie and foreboding. An umbrella of oak trees, hundreds of years old, enveloped the entrance in near-darkness, though the day was clear and sunny.

Susan parked the car in a nearby clearing, and the three of them stepped out and looked up at what had once been a very impressive dwelling. In the center of the house was a large gable with an arched window that overlooked a porch. The porch was supported by four posts, once white, but now gray and crumbling with age.

There was a big chimney on either side, and there were many large windows with tiny panes, some of them broken. A wing, also with a chimney, extended toward the back and seemed almost as spacious as the main part of the house.

Susan was greatly disappointed, for she had not expected the house to look quite so dilapidated, though she did not say anything. With difficulty she tried to imagine Hollowhearth House bustling with activity. Now the only signs of life were the scurrying squirrels and the birds fluttering overhead. There was a certain grandeur about the place, Susan admitted to herself, but that belonged to the past.

"I know it doesn't look like much now," said Marge, noticing Susan's dejected expression. "But just wait until the gray stone has been cleaned and the trim painted and those broken windows repaired."

"I didn't mean to look so downcast," apologized Susan, adjusting her glasses and tossing her long, silky black hair away from her face. "I think Hollowhearth House has great possibilities. What's your opinion, Professor Scott?"

The young man had circled to the other side of the building and did not hear Susan's question. The girls quickly followed him, wondering what had caused his rapid disappearance.

"This must have been some house in its day," he said elatedly as Susan and Marge approached. "I never imagined there was so much of value."

"Do you really mean that?" cried Marge.

"Absolutely. If only the place had been kept in better condition. Why, there must be a gold mine in antiques!"

Randall Scott was peering through one of the grimy windows, studying the contents of the rear wing. Susan, her curiosity aroused, hurried to the next window and pressed her face against the glass.

"Hey, you two," Marge called, amused by their actions, "I have a key to the front door, you know."

"I especially want to see the library," said Susan as she followed the young professor through the old oak-paneled door and into the hallway. The air was heavy, with a musty smell, and Susan rushed over to help Marge, who was trying to open a window, but Randall Scott was two steps ahead of her and had the stuck window open with a single thrust of his strong arms.

"Whew, that's a relief!" gasped Marge. "I can just smell the mold."

"Marge, come over here and look at all these old books," Susan called from across the room. "Some of them are at least a hundred years old."

Randall Scott had already climbed the wooden

staircase to the second floor, and the girls could hear him tramping about above their heads.

"Come on up," he called in a loud voice. "You should see these Civil War uniforms."

As Susan and Marge entered one of the massive bedrooms, Professor Scott held up a long blue coat with a flowing cape, a gold buckle at the waist, and gold buttons down the front. "This is a coat worn by a member of the Union Army. Look, there is even a campaign medal pinned to the lapel." Randall Scott pointed to a rectangular pin, half blue and half gray, which adorned the heavy garment.

"Oh, how thrilling!" squealed Marge, opening a closet door. "Look at how many gowns are in here."

Randall Scott's fascination grew as they continued to investigate the other rooms. He became more and more encouraging about renovating the house.

"The project is certainly a worthwhile one," he said to Susan and Marge. "Thanks for introducing me to it. I'm certain that the Historical Society will help out financially. A great deal of money will be needed to redo the entire building."

Susan was amazed at how spacious Hollowhearth House was. In the rear wing was an immense room with floor-length velvet draperies and a large, exquisite crystal chandelier. Presumably this room had been a combination dining room and ballroom, although to dance there now would seem very out of place. The wallpaper was completely torn off in many spots, the wooden floor sagged, and large cobwebs hung from the ceiling and furniture.

There was indeed a valuable array of antiques. Cupboards of delicate china stood in nearly every corner of the ground floor. Each room contained lovely hand-carved furniture, some of the pieces broken and all of them extremely dirty. The library alone was worth thousands of dollars.

"Going through every room will take ages," Marge said. "Why, look at all we've found already. Let's go back upstairs and look at those lovely gowns."

"The Historical Society will be overjoyed," commented Professor Scott as the trio once more ascended the stairs. "It's a shame that Bruce Webb let the place get into such poor condition."

The young man wandered off into another room, while the girls returned to where the dusty gowns hung in a closet. Suddenly they heard his footsteps in the hall, and in another second he was standing in the doorway, an expression of disbelief on his handsome face.

"Bruce Webb," he blurted. "He's standing on the front lawn. He isn't dead! He's alive!"

## Chapter IV

### *Strange Circumstances*

THE YOUNG PROFESSOR pointed toward the front of the house. Susan Sand ran to a window, threw it open, and thrust out her head. Standing on the weed-choked lawn, a suitcase in his hand, was a tall, lean figure clad in a dark topcoat. After fumbling for several moments in one pocket, he drew out what appeared to be a key and quickly approached the front door.

Susan was motionless. She knew that this undoubtedly was Bruce Webb, for Professor Scott had known the man too well to be mistaken. As she studied him from the window, she was struck by the expression of cunning on his thin face. In another moment he was gone from her view and she heard the downstairs door open and then slam shut.

Randall Scott, having regained some of his composure, walked to the top of the stairs and hurried down, Susan and Marge close behind him. The man was removing his coat, but he stopped and spun around, meeting the professor with penetrating eyes.

"What's this?" he cried. "What are you doing here?"

"I might ask you the very same question," Randall Scott replied. "If I believed in such things, I'd swear you were a ghost."

The man almost smiled, and his expression softened, but only for an instant. "This is my house, Randall," he coldly replied.

"You're supposed to be dead—drowned," stammered Marge. "How did you . . . ?"

"That's none of your business," was the curt answer. "As you can see, I am very much alive."

While the trio stared at him in silence, he pulled a ragged piece of paper from an inside pocket and held it up. "This is the deed to the house, and it's in my name. I've had it for over five years, and I assure you that it's perfectly genuine. Therefore, I must consider you all trespassers."

"Doesn't our former friendship mean anything to you, Bruce?" asked Randall Scott quietly.

Bruce Webb's answer to Professor Scott was abrupt and uncompromising, for he merely opened the door and motioned the three of them to leave.

"There's no use arguing with him," Susan whispered.

Professor Scott, realizing that Susan was right, made no attempt at further conversation. Reluctantly he walked onto the wooden porch and down the steps, Marge following at his heels. Susan, however, stopped directly in front of Bruce Webb and boldly met his penetrating glare. Her green eyes sparkled with determination.

"May I see that deed?" she coolly asked.

Bruce Webb hesitated and stared at the bespectacled girl before him. Then, reaching into his pocket once more, he thrust the paper into her hand. As he stretched his arm toward her, his coat sleeve hiked up, and Susan noticed that there was an elastic bandage on his wrist.

"I sprained my wrist badly," he snapped, yanking the sleeve down again.

"I'm sorry to hear that," she murmured, very much puzzled at his anger. Then, dropping her eyes to the document, she scanned it swiftly. There seemed to be no doubt about its authenticity.

"It's no forgery, if that's what you're thinking," Bruce Webb said.

Susan made no reply but politely handed the deed back to him and joined her friends on the porch. The door slammed loudly behind her.

"What do I do now?" Marge said dejectedly. "The house belongs to him. He'll never consent to its being restored. All those lovely antiques will just sit there and gather dust."

"Or be sold for profit," added Susan.

As they started down the road toward the car, Susan could not dispel the feeling that Bruce Webb's return to Hollowhearth involved more than a matter of his right to the property. His reluctance to talk about his startling return was unnatural.

"You know, you both may think that I'm imagining something," she said, "but I think that Bruce Webb is afraid and that he's hiding his fear by trying to frighten us."

"Well, he certainly frightened me," replied Marge. "How can a man who has been proven to be dead just suddenly come back?"

"There are several possibilities, of course," replied Susan. "Either he was not on that ship when it went down, or he was pulled from the sea and kept his rescue a secret."

"Sue, I'm beginning to wonder if there isn't some connection between Bruce Webb's return and the man who followed you into Marge's store yesterday morning," said Professor Scott, his brows knit in thought. "Perhaps the man was Bruce Webb himself."

"No, he wasn't. That man was stocky and hunched over. Bruce Webb is tall and thin," said Susan with certainty.

No one spoke for the next few minutes as they trudged through tall weeds on the way to Susan's car.

Finally Randall Scott said, "What do you suggest we do, Sue?"

"First of all, I think Marge should contact her lawyer as soon as possible to see what the legal implications are," the black-haired girl replied. "I doubt that there is much he can do, but at least it's worth a try."

"I'll do as you say and call him just as soon as I get home," replied Marge. "Oh, how I hate to tell my mother about this! She has been counting so much on our owning Hollowhearth."

During the drive back to Irongate University, Susan was unusually quiet. Her mind was trying to sort out the events that had so suddenly cast doubt on the future of Hollowhearth House and robbed Marge of her rightful inheritance. What lay behind Bruce

Webb's disappearance, and why had he returned at this particular time?

"What is going on in that clever brain of yours, Susan?" asked Professor Scott as he stepped out of her car. "You've hardly spoken during the last hour."

"I'm afraid that my mind is all muddled right now," she replied, "but there is one thing that I wish you would do. Please try and find out as much about Bruce Webb's past as you can. See if you can dig up any old correspondence from him or perhaps contact people who may have known him."

"I'll certainly do what I can, but don't be too optimistic. It's been years since I had anything to do with the man."

Randall Scott waved good-bye, and Susan continued on to Marge's house. After trying to bolster her friend's sagging spirits, and eliciting a promise that the girl would call her after she had contacted her lawyer, Susan left Marge at her door. Five minutes later she drove into the driveway of her own big stone house.

After hurrying up the steps and into the house, Susan went directly to the library, where her Aunt Adele spent most of her time.

"Susan, what's the trouble?" asked the tall, slender Professor Sand, her alert gray eyes studying the girl. "You look concerned. Did you go to Hollowhearth with Marge and Randall Scott?"

As quickly and clearly as possible Susan related the story of Bruce Webb's return to Hollowhearth House. When she had finished, Professor Sand sat for several moments in thoughtful silence.

"Then Bruce Webb was never on the ship in the first place," she said finally. "And he doesn't want anyone to know what really did happen."

"That is exactly the way the three of us felt," replied Susan. "And a very queer thing happened as he was showing me the deed. He got angry when I noticed a bandage on his wrist."

"A bandage on his wrist?"

There was no doubt in Susan's mind that her quick-minded aunt had immediately seen the implications of Bruce Webb's anger.

"Yes," she said to her aunt's unspoken remark, "I think he might have a tattoo like that of the man who followed me into Marge's store."

"You are probably right," replied Professor Sand. "There is no other logical reason for him to have lost his temper over your noticing his bandaged wrist."

Susan and her aunt continued their discussion of the case during dinner. Mrs. Agnes Draper, their cook and housekeeper, lived in the Sand home and became caught up in everything Susan did. She listened with rapt attention as the young sleuth related the day's events to her.

"You be careful, Susan," she warned in an anxious voice. "That Bruce Webb sounds dangerous to me."

When Susan retired late that night to her room, her marmalade cat was reclining comfortably on her bed.

"What do you think, Icky?" she asked the fluffy animal. "I named you after the Pharaoh Ikhnaton Amenhotep IV, because the Egyptians thought cats were in possession of some secret knowledge. That's why they worshiped and even mummified their cats."

Icky purred loudly as Susan stroked his silky fur, but he could not shed any light on the mystery at Hollowhearth House.

Despite the turmoil of the last twelve hours, Susan fell asleep immediately and did not stir until the morning light streamed through the trees outside her bedroom window. Just as she was going downstairs to breakfast, the front doorbell rang.

"Who on earth could be calling at this hour?" asked Professor Sand from the library.

Susan opened the door to find a rather elderly woman, plump and pleasant in appearance, standing on the porch.

"Why, Mrs. Manning!" said Susan in surprise, greeting their former housekeeper cordially. "What brings you here so early? Is something the matter?"

"I know this is a terrible hour to come ringing people's doorbells, but I had to talk to someone," the woman replied, a serious expression on her usually jolly face.

Susan escorted Mrs. Manning to the couch in the living room and sat down beside her as Professor Sand came in from the library and Mrs. Draper from the kitchen.

"You see, it all involves this man who called me last night about working for him at Hollowhearth House," began Mrs. Manning.

"Hollowhearth House!" was the unanimous cry.

"Do you mean that Bruce Webb called you last night and asked you to work for him?" Susan asked in disbelief.

"Why, yes," Mrs. Manning replied. "He said he'd seen my ad in the newspaper. How do you know his name?"

Briefly Susan related the events of the day before.

"I thought there was something strange about him," Mrs. Manning said. "I went out there and told him I'd take the job, but after I got to thinking about it, I wondered if I had done a foolish thing."

"What exactly does he want you to do?" Professor Sand asked.

"Well, he wants me to work only a few hours a day, just to cook his supper. I'm to get to the house at four-thirty and leave as soon as the dishes are done."

"How very odd!" exclaimed Susan. "What else did he say?"

"First of all, he told me never to come to work except at the hours agreed upon. Then he made me promise never to enter the rear wing, but always to stay in the kitchen."

"Oh, my," said Mrs. Draper in a whisper. "I would never take that job, Emily, if I were you. To be all alone in that big house with Bruce Webb, miles away from town—"

"But I won't be all alone, Agnes," Mrs. Manning interrupted. "At least not the entire time. He also hired a Michael Leeds as gardener."

"Then he certainly intends to try to fix the place up," Susan mused. "But why would he keep you from going into the rear wing?"

"I don't know, dear," sighed Mrs. Manning. "But for the salary he's going to give me, I really shouldn't complain about anything. Why, I nearly passed out when he told me how much he was willing to pay for just a few hours' work."

"He knew he would never get a soul to work for him way out there if he didn't pay well," stated Mrs. Draper vigorously. "Perhaps you should call him and say you changed your mind."

"But I must have the job, Agnes, and with the way I've been feeling lately, a few hours' work a day at such good pay is just what I need." Mrs. Manning fingered her pocketbook nervously. "What do you think I should do, Susan?"

"If you were going to be alone in the house, I would tell you not to take the job," Susan earnestly replied. "But because the salary is so good and you will be working only a few hours a day, I think you should try it. After all, I can't imagine why Bruce Webb should want to harm you."

"I think you are right," replied Mrs. Manning, relaxing a bit. "I knew I was just making too much of the whole thing. And now I really must go. I've taken up too much of your time already."

"Make sure you let us know how you are getting on," said Aunt Adele as Mrs. Manning descended the porch steps.

"I will. And don't worry about me," she called back.

After the woman had left, Mrs. Draper could not hide her concern. "Are you certain you have done a wise thing, Susan?" she asked searchingly. "You've taken on the responsibility for Mrs. Manning's safety."

"I know. And I'm already beginning to worry.

Perhaps I made a serious mistake. If anything should happen to Mrs. Manning, I would never forgive myself."

Mrs. Draper went back to the kitchen to continue making breakfast, and Susan remained motionless on the sofa, her forehead tense with worry.

## Chapter V

## *At the Steamship Office*

"NOW don't worry about it too much, Susan," Professor Sand said soothingly. "Agnes Draper frets about everything. Emily Manning has a good head on her shoulders. But," she added, "it's just that we know so little about Bruce Webb."

"And what we do know isn't very comforting. Oh, Aunt Adele, I think I'll go after Mrs. Manning and tell her not to take the job."

Susan ran through the door and down the walk, but the woman had already boarded a bus, which was just pulling away from the curb at the corner.

"I was too late," Susan said ruefully as she reentered the living room. "I'll wait until she gets home and then give her a call."

Before Professor Sand could reply, the telephone rang and Susan sprang to answer it. Marge Halloran was on the other end of the line.

"I contacted my lawyer as you suggested, Sue," she began. "He doesn't sound very hopeful. I'm afraid the law is on Bruce Webb's side unless I can somehow prove that he tricked my grandfather."

"I was afraid of that," said Susan. "But don't give up yet. After all, Bruce Webb hasn't been back in Thornewood twenty-four hours."

"What are you cooking up, Sue?" Marge asked, a note of hope in her voice.

"Well, if your mother will take the bookstore for today, I thought you and I might do some sleuthing—in New York City."

"Sue, I'd love to—but I can't. We have to take inventory at the store today. Besides, what's in New York?"

"Perhaps a clue to Bruce Webb's return from the 'dead.' I thought I would visit the Venezuelan Steamship Office and see if they have any information on the sinking of the ship he was supposed to have been on. What was the ship's name?"

"*El Cometa*," said Marge.

"'The Comet,' in Spanish," murmured Susan, making a mental note of the name.

"Yes, the Comet," returned Marge, managing a slight laugh. "Sue, I can't thank you enough for what you are trying to do. I only wish that I could go with you."

"I'll call you when I get back. Meanwhile, try not to worry."

After hanging up, Susan waited several moments and then dialed a number.

"Who are you calling, Susan?" Aunt Adele asked.

"I thought I'd ask Professor Scott if he's managed to find out anything about Bruce Webb," she replied.

"I suppose I should give him a chance to call me, but he's so busy he may not have had time."

To Susan's disappointment, Professor Scott was not yet in his office. Not wanting to waste any more time, the young author ate a hasty breakfast and decided to start for New York City immediately.

"Maybe I'm going on a wild goose chase," Susan said as she donned a green leather jacket. "But a visit to the steamship office might shed some light on why Bruce Webb was listed as drowned."

"You should follow up any clue, Susan," replied Professor Sand. "Sleuthing is similar to scholarly research. You have to dig to get the facts."

Susan bade her aunt good-bye and set out for the big city, which was about twenty miles from Thornewood. Because her publisher was located there, Susan was used to the route into midtown Manhattan, but today she had to drive almost to the end of the island to reach her destination.

After turning off the highway, she drove along the Hudson River past piers and wharfs and ships at dock until she arrived at the Venezuelan Steamship Office. The slender raven-haired girl paid no attention to several longshoremen who were watching as she alighted from her car and quickly entered the low building.

"Can I help you, miss?" asked a pleasant man seated behind a desk.

"Yes, I'm looking for some information on a ship called *El Cometa*," Susan replied in a businesslike manner. "I understand that the ship sank on its journey back from Caracas, Venezuela."

Susan's words had a strange effect on the man, for the polite smile quickly faded from his face and his dark eyes stared at her until she felt uncomfortable.

"*El Cometa*?" he said after a long silence. "Why are you interested?"

"I would like to get a list of the passengers who were on board when it went down," Susan replied cautiously.

While she conversed with the man, she noticed that he kept glancing at her hands. Then in an embarrassed tone he asked her what time it was. Susan looked at her watch, told him the time, and then saw, to her amazement, that a large clock on the wall told the time exactly.

"Whatever is the matter with him?" she mused to herself.

"I don't know if I will be able to find that information for you," the man said. "I will have to look at our records."

Rising from his desk, he disappeared into another room and was gone for what seemed to Susan to be a very long time. From the other room she could hear the sound of voices speaking in Spanish. There seemed to be an argument in progress, for the voices grew louder and more animated. Several times she could make out the words *la marca.*

"*La marca* means 'mark' or 'sign' in Spanish," said Susan to herself.

As she was mulling the matter over, the man reappeared, carrying a large black book.

"I'm very sorry to have kept you waiting so long," he said with forced courtesy. "But you see, you are the second person today who has asked us about *El Cometa.* That is a very unusual situation, is it not?" The man smiled at Susan, but there was no humor in his face.

"Yes, very unusual," Susan replied. "Who else was asking about the ship?"

"I do not know his name, miss," was the evasive reply. "I showed him the very same book I am showing you. That is all I can tell you."

"Was he a hunched-over man in a trenchcoat?" she asked excitedly.

"I cannot tell you, miss," he replied, and Susan saw that his hands had begun to tremble.

She adjusted her glasses and studied the page the man had opened for her. There it was! The name of Bruce Webb, Hollowhearth House, Thornewood, U.S.A., staring at her in bold letters. He was listed among the drowned.

Trying not to show her excitement, Susan thanked the man and left the office, convinced that she could obtain no further information. Once on the street, she felt a sense of elation.

"*La marca!*" she said to herself. "The mark! I'm certain the man with the strange tattoo was here before me, and that frightened clerk was trying to see if I had the same mark on my wrist. That's why he asked me for the time. He wanted me to pull up my sleeve to look at my watch!"

Susan backed her car away from the steamship office and started toward home.

"Oh, what have I stumbled into?" she said aloud.

## Chapter VI

## *A Valuable Clue*

"WHAT have I stumbled into?" Susan Sand repeated to herself as she drove through the heavy traffic of downtown Manhattan. "Bruce Webb was definitely listed as a passenger on *El Cometa*, but why wasn't he on the ship when it sank? And did the man in the trenchcoat ask about him?"

With these thoughts spinning in her brain, the young sleuth left the great metropolis and soon was on her way to Thornewood.

"I'll go directly to Irongate and tell Professor Scott about this," she said decisively as she stepped on the accelerator of her car. "He'll be fascinated when I tell him about the clerk and the word *la marca*."

The campus of Irongate was humming with activity when Susan entered the gates, parked her car, and hurried to Piper Hall.

"Oh, I hope Professor Scott isn't too busy to see me," she said anxiously to herself, climbing the stairs past the little stained-glass window which was in some unaccountable way connected with the mystery. Susan glanced quickly at the coat of arms and wondered if Professor Scott had uncovered any new information about the emblem of the black bird.

As she reached the top of the stairway and crossed to the secretary's desk, the young professor's voice could be heard coming from the inner office. Susan sat down patiently to wait, for the secretary said he was in conference with a student.

By the time Randall Scott was ready to see her, Susan had composed her thoughts and was able to explain to him clearly what had occurred at the steamship office. She also mentioned Bruce Webb's anger when she noticed his bandaged wrist.

"You are certainly talented at uncovering facts, Susan," said Professor Scott with a smile. "Although we have no proof, I'm inclined to think that Bruce Webb has a tattoo like the one you saw on the intruder's wrist. That would explain the bandage. The clerk in the steamship office wanted to see if you had the same mark before he gave you any information."

"Yes, he consulted with someone in the back room, and the words *la marca* were repeated several times," Susan replied.

"Then that escutcheon of the black bird must represent something vitally important," said Professor Scott, pacing back and forth.

"Have you been able to do any research on the window?" Susan asked expectantly.

"I've been too busy, Sue," he replied, running his fingers through his wavy brown hair. "But I think it would be a good idea to search this old house, especially the attic. Maybe we'll discover what former family installed that window. I did find something, however, that I'm certain you will find interesting."

Going to his desk, Randall Scott removed a large pile of papers from a drawer and laid them on the top of the desk.

"I looked through these just before you arrived," he stated. "They're old letters. There is one particular item which tells us something about Bruce Webb."

"Why, this is a newspaper clipping from a Venezuelan newspaper," said Susan, scanning the piece. "It's in Spanish."

"Yes. I had completely forgotten about that article. Unfortunately, the accompanying letter was lost."

"The entire piece is about Bruce Webb and his marriage to Teresa Crowden, the daughter of a wealthy family living in Caracas," cried Susan jubilantly. "The date is a little over a year ago."

Fingering the item thoughtfully and adjusting her glasses, the young sleuth carefully reread the clipping. "Professor Scott, this may be an important lead. Can you remember what was in the accompanying letter?"

"I'm sorry, Sue," Randall Scott replied. "I get so much mail, I have trouble remembering a letter from one day to the next. But you can see that Bruce Webb still considered himself to be a friend of mine when he sent me that clipping."

"If he married this Teresa Crowden, where is she now?" said Susan.

Professor Scott shook his head slowly from side to side. "With the way Bruce Webb has changed, there is no telling what may have happened to her. But we have made an important discovery about Webb's past. If he was involved with this Crowden family, perhaps they can give us some information about him. At least it's worth a try."

"What about Professor Endicott?" Susan cried out. "He will have arrived in South America by now. We could send him a cablegram and ask him to do some investigating."

"Of course," replied Randall Scott, snapping his fingers. "Dr. Endicott was going to Venezuela! In fact, if I remember correctly, he'll be staying in Caracas."

"Oh, dear," reflected Susan. "I suppose we would be imposing on him if we asked him to take time looking up the Crowdens."

"If I know Giles Endicott, he'll do all he can to help us. The only drawback will be his schedule. I know he plans to take several trips while in the country."

"And even after we reach him, he would need time to gather information," Susan added. "The clue is a slim one but worth following."

"After what you told me about your visit to New York, things are not at a complete standstill," Professor Scott replied. "You're not letting the grass grow, as the saying goes."

"And now Dr. Endicott has become a partner, only he doesn't know it yet," said Susan with an impish smile. "Let's get a cablegram off to Caracas right now."

Susan took a pad from the desk and wrote out the message. "How does this sound, Professor?" she asked. "Did I include everything?"

Randall Scott took the paper and read aloud:

"REQUIRE INFORMATION CROWDEN FAMILY CARACAS STOP DID BRUCE WEBB MARRY DAUGHTER STOP INFORMATION VITAL
SUSAN SAND AND RANDALL SCOTT"

"I couldn't have put it better myself," he said, picking up the telephone and dialing Western Union. After dictating the cablegram and giving his own name and address, he replaced the receiver and sat back in his chair.

"Let's hope that will bring results," he said, scanning the clipping again.

As Professor Scott was rereading the item, the door to his office suddenly burst open and, to the amazement of the two of them, Marge Halloran came in, sobbing.

"I—I knew I would find you here, Sue," she stammered.

"Why, Marge, what is it?" cried Susan, rushing to her.

"I'm afraid I just did a very foolish thing," the redheaded girl said. "I went to Hollowhearth House to see Bruce Webb."

"Oh, my," said Susan. "Whatever did he do?"

"Oh, Sue, he was awful." Marge sat down in a leather chair and buried her face in her hands. "I only wanted to talk to him about restoring the house. I thought maybe we could work something out, even though the place is in his name."

"What did he say?" Randall Scott asked gently.

"Oh, he got so angry!" cried Marge. "I just stood

there on the porch while he ranted and raved about how the property was his and I was a trespasser and I had no right to keep pestering him. Then he grabbed my arm and said, 'Get out of here, you little snoop!' And with that he gave me a push and I almost fell down the steps. As I ran toward my car, he shouted after me, 'There's a way of getting rid of you!' "

"This is becoming more serious all the time," Susan stated with a worried frown. "Bruce Webb has no reason to act like this unless he has something to hide."

"Well, regardless of what he meant by that statement, you mustn't go near Hollowhearth again, Marge," Professor Scott said emphatically. "There is no telling what he might do."

"Yes," said Susan in a serious tone. "He's made a real threat."

"Oh dear!" wailed Marge. "What does he mean by 'there's a way of getting rid' of me?"

## Chapter VII

## *A Helpful Gardener*

"MARGE, don't let Bruce Webb frighten you," said Susan Sand soothingly. "He was only trying to keep you away from Hollowhearth House."

"But why?" asked Marge, wiping her eyes with her handkerchief.

"I don't know yet, but I intend to find out," Susan replied in a determined voice. "Right now I think you should go home and try to put this experience out of your mind. Bruce Webb won't harm you as long as you stay away from Hollowhearth."

"Yes, I must get back to the bookstore and relieve mother," said Marge, rising. "I'll try to take your advice, Sue."

After thanking the pair for their help, Marge Halloran left the office in a much calmer state. Randall Scott, who had an important faculty meeting, escorted Susan to her car and, with a parting admonition to be careful, strode purposefully across the campus.

"Considering the way Bruce Webb treated Marge, I can't help feeling that Mrs. Manning might be in danger," mused the young sleuth as she drove from the campus. "Perhaps, if I am very cautious, I could do some snooping without being caught."

After several moments of deliberation, Susan decided she would go to Hollowhearth House herself and investigate. She knew the move was a daring one, but her concern for her friends outweighed all danger. The many trees and bushes on the property would afford protection from being discovered.

The afternoon was waning when Susan turned onto the cliff road that led to Hollowhearth Hill. Her only misgiving was that she might have been wise to wait until Professor Scott could accompany her.

"He leads a busy life," she told herself. "I shouldn't expect him to worry about me."

Once on the private dirt road, the car bumped and jolted its way along. Not a soul was in sight. Because the area was heavily wooded, very little of the remaining sunlight filtered down to the road.

As soon as Hollowhearth Hill came into view, Susan decided to park her car in a secluded spot and travel the rest of the way on foot. When she was convinced that her car could not be seen from the road, she started quickly up the hill.

Staying in the shelter of the trees, Susan walked rapidly but began to slow her pace as she neared the house. Suddenly she spotted a man on the lawn about fifty feet away. The raven-haired girl drew in a deep breath and advanced nearer to the figure. He was bending over, doing some work, his back toward Susan.

Well hidden behind a huge weeping willow tree,

she waited silently for several moments. As the man continued to work he turned slightly, giving Susan an opportunity to see his face. He was a person of at least sixty, rugged and lean.

"He must be Michael Leeds, the gardener Bruce Webb hired," Susan told herself, noticing hedge shears in his hand.

Susan moved a little to one side in order to see the man better. As she did so, she stepped on a large dry branch, which gave a loud crack. The man whirled around at the sound and stared directly at her.

"Are you lost?" he asked suddenly.

"No," replied Susan. "I'm a friend of Mrs. Manning. She is to start working today as Mr. Webb's cook."

"Don't think she'll like it," the man replied. He continued to study Susan with his questioning gray eyes.

"Why do you say that?" she asked.

"He's a strange one, miss. But how come you know him?"

Before answering, Susan wondered how much she should divulge. If she could befriend this person, he might prove to be a valuable ally. He was in a good spot to know what was going on at Hollowhearth House.

"My name is Susan Sand," she said cordially, extending her hand.

"Oh, you're that new author I've been hearing so much about," replied Michael Leeds, shaking Susan's hand warmly. "I'm very pleased to meet you. I haven't been able to find a copy of *The Bony Finger* yet."

"I'd be glad to give you an autographed copy," the young author generously replied.

"I sure would appreciate that, Miss Sand," said Michael Leeds, his face breaking into a smile.

Briefly Susan explained about Marge's inheritance and plans for the house. He moved over to her, glancing back over his shoulder several times before speaking again.

"He only hired me yesterday afternoon, Miss Sand, so I really don't know much about him," Mr. Leeds continued. "The money was so good I jumped at the opportunity."

"That's exactly what Mrs. Manning told me," said Susan. "Money certainly doesn't seem to be a problem for him."

"Well, I think he's afraid of something," stated the gardener in a dramatic tone.

"Afraid of something? What makes you think that?" Susan asked with growing interest.

The gardener studied Susan intently, as if appraising her ability to keep a confidence.

"I know that I can trust you, Miss Sand," he said presently, "but I don't want Bruce Webb to see me talking to you." His voice was so low Susan could barely hear him. "There's something mighty funny going on inside that house."

Susan's heart began to pound. She felt that Michael Leeds knew more about the old house than she had expected.

"Why do you think that?" Susan asked, attempting to sound calm.

"Well, first of all, when he hired me, he told me never to enter the house. He told me not even to set foot on the porch."

"If he feels that way, why do you think he hired you at all?"

Michael Leeds fumbled several moments with his shears. "That's the funniest part of the whole thing, Miss Sand," he said finally. "I asked him the very same question. At first he got mad. Then he said, 'Listen here, Leeds, your job is to take care of the outside of this house. The inside is my business and nobody else's!' "

"But why is he so concerned with the grounds? I doubt if he cares at all about the house itself."

"I think it's all a front," the gardener whispered. "He figures if the house looks nice from the outside, nobody will care what goes on inside. Otherwise, he wouldn't care whether or not he had a gardener."

"I think you are absolutely right, Mr. Leeds," Susan replied. "That is a very plausible explanation."

"There's another queer thing that happened this morning," he continued. "I'd almost forgotten about it."

"What was that?"

"Well, I was around the back of the place, right by the rear wing, mowing the lawn. I stopped to rest a minute and just happened to glance up at the window. Bruce Webb was in the back room, acting kind of funny."

"Funny? What was he doing?"

"He was reaching up into the air."

"Reaching into the air! What was he reaching for?" asked Susan.

"Nothing that I could see," replied Michael Leeds, scratching his head and frowning slightly. "Nothing that I could see," he repeated. "Anyway, when he saw me, he ran over and pulled down the shade."

"Did he say anything?"

The gardener shook his head. "Not a word, but he looked awful mad."

"I hope he doesn't see us standing here talking," said Susan, moving farther back into the woods. "Is there anything else strange about him?"

"Well, last evening, it was almost midnight, I had to come back because I left my keys in the tool shed. He didn't know I was around. He went somewhere in his car, a yellow convertible."

"At midnight?"

"Yep, that's right. He must have money, because that's a mighty expensive new car he's driving."

"Oh, I do wish I hadn't advised Mrs. Manning to take the job," moaned Susan. "This is becoming far more serious than I had bargained for."

"Well, Miss Sand, as long as he pays our wages, there is no use complaining. But I'm glad I don't have to work inside."

"Mr. Leeds, I can't thank you enough. You have been very helpful," said Susan. "If anything else unusual should happen, please contact me at this address." Susan handed him one of her little white cards. Printed in gold letters were her name, address, and telephone number.

"I'll make certain, Mr. Leeds, that you get an autographed copy of *The Bony Finger.*"

"I sure would appreciate that," the gardener replied enthusiastically. "I've heard so much about the book already."

"I know you won't say anything to Mr. Webb about our talk," she cautioned. "And now I think I had better get back to my car. I've taken enough chances being seen."

"You can trust me," Michael Leeds assured her. "And I'll try to keep my eye on Mrs. Manning for you."

Susan started for her car but had not gone more than a hundred yards when she heard the sound of a motor. There was a car moving carefully along the rocky road.

"It's Mrs. Manning," said Susan. "Thank heavens I'll have a chance to talk with her before she enters the house."

Mrs. Manning stopped her car when she saw Susan coming toward her. "Why, Susan, what on earth are you doing here?" she asked.

Quickly Susan explained why she had returned to the house, and described her conversation with Michael Leeds. She felt that she must be completely truthful about the possible dangers that lay inside the house.

"I really think you should give up the job, Mrs. Manning," she warned. "I know the money is important to you, but you must be careful, too."

"Maybe you are right, Susan," replied the cook. "But I will be in the house for only a few hours a day. Besides, Mr. Leeds will be working about the place."

"Well, that makes me feel a little better," replied Susan.

"Don't worry about me, dear. I can take care of myself."

"I'm sure you can, Mrs. Manning," Susan replied. "But I'll worry just the same. Mr. Leeds thinks there's something 'mighty funny' going on in that house. You must be very cautious."

"I will be, Susan. And I'll keep my eyes open for anything that seems suspicious to me."

Susan thanked the woman and started back toward her car. Dusk was falling, and several dim lights flickered through the windows of Hollowhearth House. As Susan hurried down the road, she glanced back over her shoulder. Large oak trees almost completely blocked her view of the front of the structure. Only one window could be seen through the woods. Suddenly Susan stopped. Was that something moving at the window? Peering through her glasses, she tried to make out what the movement might be, but evening shadows prevented her from distinguishing anything.

"Oh, I hope that Bruce Webb didn't see me," she thought, recalling his threat to Marge.

Susan's car stood in the secluded spot where she had left it. Climbing in, she started the motor and turned on the headlights. The main highway was not far, but the thought that Bruce Webb might have been watching her from the window made her wish that she were not in such a lonely place.

She had not gone more than an eighth of a mile when the headlights of another car were reflected in her rear-view mirror. A yellow convertible with the top down was following her. Bruce Webb was at the wheel!

## Chapter VIII

## *A Confrontation*

BRUCE WEBB made no attempt to pass Susan Sand. Several times she slowed down, but the yellow convertible slowed down also.

"I can't imagine what he hopes to gain by following me," she said to herself. "Perhaps this is his way of telling me to keep away from Hollowhearth Hill."

There was no doubt in Susan's mind that Bruce Webb was resorting to scare tactics in his effort to prevent people from coming to Hollowhearth House. His headlights were reflected in her rear-view mirror so brightly that the glare made driving difficult. Because the road to the old house was private, there was no traffic until the main highway. Legally, Bruce Webb could force anyone off the road if he so desired. Susan was a trespasser.

"He could even go to the police," she murmured under her breath, "and there isn't a thing anyone could do to stop him."

Susan considered trying to lose her pursuer in the traffic, once she had reached the highway, but her curiosity overcame any fear she may have had. She continued in the center lane at a moderate speed, the yellow convertible keeping pace behind. Bruce Webb's face, reflected in her rear-view mirror, was distorted with anger. His hair was disheveled, and he leaned over the wheel like a racing driver crossing the finish line.

"I'll head straight for home," thought Susan. "If he wants to confront me, he will have to do it there. I only hope he doesn't give Mrs. Draper a heart attack."

All the way to Thornewood the spunky girl thought about what she would say to her pursuer if he followed her right to her house. From his appearance it seemed likely he would be difficult to talk with rationally.

The streetlights were already on when Susan turned into a side street and then onto the road where her house was located. She had forgotten what time it was and that Professor Sand would be at the university for an evening class. She would have to face Bruce Webb alone in the deserted house, for when she pulled into the driveway, she suddenly remembered that Mrs. Draper had the evening off. There were no lights shining in any of the windows.

"Perhaps I have done a foolish thing," she thought, momentarily apprehensive. "But no, I will face this man and try to talk some sense to him!"

Susan jumped out of her car just as Bruce Webb drove right up into the driveway behind her. Pretending to ignore him, she fumbled for her key and entered the house.

"You just wait a minute!" he cried, forcing his way

into the wide entrance foyer and slamming the door before Susan could turn on the light.

"What do you want?" Susan asked in a steady voice. "You've been following me all the way from Hollow-hearth Hill. Why?"

Susan could barely see his face in the dark. As she talked, she walked over to the wall switch and turned on the light. Bruce Webb stood backed against the white door, his bandaged wrist showing plainly. His face was pale with anger, and for a few moments he said nothing. He glanced around at the book-lined walls and then stared angrily at Susan.

Finally, advancing toward his confronter, he said menacingly, "I'm getting mighty impatient with you. I'm warning you for the last time to stay away from Hollowhearth!"

"Then why don't you call the police?" replied Susan, in a sudden burst of anger usually foreign to her nature. "What are you so afraid of that makes you act like a fugitive? What are you doing in that house?"

Bruce Webb seemed stunned by this slight, bespectacled girl confronting him in such a forthright manner. He knew she had called his bluff and he must use another tactic. His manner became calmer and his voice more subdued.

"Now look here," he began, "you and I have misunderstood each other all along. I just got back from a very tiring trip, and I'm not myself. When I saw a bunch of strangers in my house, naturally I got mad."

"Mr. Webb," Susan replied, her mind working quickly, "you must understand that everyone thought you were dead, that you had gone down on *El*

*Cometa.* Marge Halloran had her heart set on owning and restoring Hollowhearth House. Your return was a great shock to all of us."

Bruce Webb looked perplexed. He saw that Susan did not frighten easily.

Realizing his confusion, Susan decided on another bold move. "Tell me, Mr. Webb," she continued, "did you marry Teresa Crowden while you were in Venezuela?"

The question had an unexpected effect on the man. Instead of becoming angry again, he stared at Susan for several seconds without speaking. She continued her questioning.

"What happened on *El Cometa?* Did you escape from the ship, or were you never on board in the first place? The man in the Venezuelan Steamship Office seemed upset when I asked him if I could see the passenger list. He said someone else had been in that day, asking the same question I did."

At these words Bruce Webb's expression changed from one of confusion to one of fear. Without uttering a word, he turned, ran through the door, and fled to his car. Susan stood in the doorway, looking after him, as he backed out of the driveway and drove off.

"Well," she said out loud, "I certainly touched a sore spot. I hope I didn't reveal too much. If I can keep him on the defensive, I'll still have the upper hand."

As Susan went into her study, her mind was trying to sort out what had just happened. Events had taken a very different turn from what she had anticipated.

Now she was glad that her visit to Hollowhearth House had been discovered, for she had learned that Bruce Webb was indeed frightened.

"Perhaps the hunched-over man in the trenchcoat is an enemy of Bruce Webb's rather than an ally—but then, what about the bandage on his wrist? Does he have the same tattoo? He seemed the most upset when I mentioned my trip to the steamship office."

While Susan continued to ask herself questions, she suddenly realized how hungry she was. Icky came meowing from the kitchen, asking for his dinner.

"Come, Icky," she said, bending down and giving him a kiss, "I'm hungry too."

While she was feeding Ikhnaton and preparing her own dinner, her mind worked feverishly. "At least I have learned several important facts, even if I don't understand what they might mean," she thought. "I must get in touch with Professor Scott and see what he has to say."

Susan picked up the telephone and dialed the professor's home. He took so long in answering that she thought for a time he was not there. When he finally did respond, he sounded out of breath.

"I was up on a ladder in my library, getting down a book on coats of arms," he explained. "I was trying to find the black bird perched on a golden crown, but there is no such escutcheon in the book. I called you an hour ago and got no answer."

Quickly Susan explained about her trip to Hollowhearth House and her encounter with Bruce Webb.

"You surely do take chances, Susan," he scolded.

"It was worth it," she assured him. "We are right in thinking that Bruce Webb is frightened about whatever happened in Venezuela."

"You mean you were right," Randall Scott replied. "You were the one who realized he was afraid."

"At least we are on the right track," said Susan modestly.

"Now I'm going to surprise you. I had a cable from Dr. Endicott. He's located the Crowden family."

"Already! That's marvelous!" cried Susan. "He certainly does work fast."

"His wire, of course, was brief, Sue. He's going to write us a letter when he has more information. The Crowdens are notorious criminals. The few people he talked with are terrified of them."

"Oh!" Susan said, drawing in her breath. "Bruce Webb married into a family of criminals! But where is his wife, and why did he come back to Hollowhearth House?"

## Chapter IX

# *The Indian Peephole*

BRUCE WEBB was a member of a family of criminals! Susan Sand, after bidding goodnight to Professor Scott, sank down on the couch in her study as she tried to disgest this vital new fact. But why had he returned to Hollowhearth House? Had there been a falling out with the Crowden family? Susan's eyes narrowed while she pondered these questions.

When Professor Sand returned from the university, the young sleuth described her visit to Hollowhearth and her confrontation with Bruce Webb. She did not want to alarm her aunt. Passing lightly over his threat to Marge, she described the man's flight in detail. At her mention of Professor Endicott's cablegram, Professor Sand's eyes widened.

"Criminals!" she exclaimed. "Susan, you must be careful."

"But he really didn't frighten me, Aunt Adele," she truthfully replied. "In fact, he was the one who was afraid."

"Nevertheless, we don't know what this involves. You say you also spoke to the gardener?"

"Yes, and he described an odd incident," replied Susan reflectively. "Mr. Leeds saw Bruce Webb through the window in the rear wing of the house. He said that he was reaching up into the air."

"Why, whatever could that mean?" Professor Sand asked.

"It may not mean anything, but there is something strange about Webb's actions. Mr. Leeds was told never to enter the house, and Mrs. Manning was ordered not to go into the rear wing. Then there is that midnight trip. Mr. Leeds had to come back to the tool shed for his keys, and he saw Bruce Webb drive off in his car."

"I'm beginning to wish that Emily Manning hadn't taken that job," said Professor Sand anxiously.

"I'll call her in the morning and tell her what we've learned," Susan replied. "I feel responsible for her safety."

The day dawned damp and sunless. Susan did not awaken until after nine o'clock, for explaining the swift progress of events to Mrs. Draper had kept her up until one o'clock.

Directly after breakfast Susan called Mrs. Manning.

"Do you know what Bruce Webb did just as I arrived yesterday?" the cook asked. "He drove off in his car and didn't return for almost two hours. His dinner was stone cold."

"He followed me home, Mrs. Manning."

"Oh my!" gasped the woman. "He seemed very

quiet when he returned. What happened? Why did he follow you?"

Quickly Susan explained the episode of the night before.

"You asked him if he married a South American girl, and he didn't answer? Well, if he has a wife, I didn't see her. I cooked enough food for two people. How such a thin man can eat so much is beyond me."

"I don't think you should stay on the job, Mrs. Manning," said Susan. "I have reason to believe that Bruce Webb might be a criminal."

"A criminal!" Mrs. Manning cried over the wire. "Well, in that case I'll have to think about remaining. I need the money, but I don't want to do anything foolish."

"Please think it over," Susan replied. "I'll be in touch with you soon."

Scarcely had Susan replaced the receiver when the telephone rang.

"Good morning, Sue," Randall Scott greeted her cheerfully. "How would you like to do some sleuthing today?"

"I'd love to!" Susan responded. "What did you have in mind?"

"I thought we could conduct a search of Piper Hall. That stained-glass window intrigues me. We might uncover something to explain the coat of arms. Most of the house has been renovated by the university, but the attic hasn't been touched in two hundred years."

"How exciting! I'll call Marge. I'm certain she'll want to help us."

"Fine. Meet me at Piper Hall in an hour."

Susan arrived at Marge's home and found her waiting on the front steps, accompanied by a tall, lean young man with curly black hair.

"This is Brian Lorenzo," Marge said as the pair climbed into Susan's car. "Brian is a student at Irongate and a member of the Thornewood Historical Society."

"I got into a conversation with Marge in her bookstore," Brian explained. "She told me about inheriting Hollowhearth House and thought I would be interested in helping to restore it."

On the way to Irongate, Marge and Brian sat fascinated as Susan described her meeting with Bruce Webb.

"And he didn't say anything when you asked about Teresa Crowden?" Marge asked.

"Not a word. Judging from the expression on his face, he was stunned that I knew anything about her."

"He has probably figured out by now that Professor Scott told you about the newspaper clipping," Marge surmised.

"Bruce Webb never realized how incriminating that item would prove to be," replied Susan, turning through the black iron gates and onto the campus.

Because it was Saturday, the campus was almost entirely deserted. A strong wind was blowing, and gloomy gray clouds covered the sun as the trio climbed from the car and headed for Piper Hall. The tall, stately poplar trees swayed like long plumes, and the ivy rustled on the walls of the surrounding buildings.

Professor Scott was waiting in his office, an astonished expression on his face as he greeted the three young people.

"I've just received another cablegram from Dr. Endicott," he rapidly informed them. "He's returning to America in several days. He has very important information about the Crowden family."

"Returning! Why can't he write to us?" asked Susan in disbelief.

"I don't know, Sue. That's all he says."

"Does he say what day he is arriving?"

"No. Just that he'll be back in a few days."

"How very odd," said Susan, half to herself. "What could be so vital that Professor Endicott feels he must come all the way back to America to tell us?"

"It's not like him to interrupt an important research trip," said Randall Scott, frowning. "We'll just have to wait until he arrives. But now let's go up to the attic and see what we can find."

Walking down the corridor and turning to the left, the others close at his heels, the young man approached a door. "Watch your step," he said. "There's no electricity up here."

"Oh, this is creepy!" whispered Marge as Professor Scott lifted the iron latch and the little wooden door swung open. Disappearing into the darkness was a flight of steep, narrow stairs. "There's hardly any light at all. We should have brought a flashlight."

"Fortunately I remembered to bring mine," answered Susan, opening her shoulder bag and withdrawing a shiny metal object. Pushing the button, the young sleuth shone the beam up the stairway, revealing another door at the top.

"Keep your heads down—especially you, Brian," said Professor Scott to the tall youth as the quartet started up into the gloom.

Once through the second door, they were assailed by a musty odor. Susan shone the bright beam around the chamber, disclosing a low, slanting roof and a grimy floor of wide wooden planks. The wall to the left of the door was of brick, and a tiny bit of daylight filtered through a small opening near the ceiling. Two windows, so dirty that almost no light could enter, were tightly shut, thus trapping the stale air.

"Let's get those windows open," said Brian, making a comical grimace. "We'll suffocate from lack of oxygen."

"Whew, that's better," exclaimed Marge with relief when, after a struggle, the stuck windows were forced up.

"That lets in a little more light, too," said Susan, flashing her beam about the room. "Oh, there's an old desk. I wonder if it contains anything."

"I've looked through the drawers, Sue, and found nothing," responded Randall Scott. "But you're welcome to search it yourself."

To Susan's disappointment, the desk proved to be entirely empty. Although she felt carefully in every drawer, and even removed the drawers and shone her light in the empty compartments, nothing was revealed.

"There isn't much up here," commented Brian disappointedly, his eyes scanning the attic. "Just a lot of dirt and cobwebs."

"Look, I think that's a ladder," cried Susan, pointing

toward the shadows on the floor under the brick wall. "What is a ladder doing up here?"

"It was probably used for mounting to the Indian peephole," Professor Scott answered, directing his finger at the tiny opening near the ceiling. "Many colonial houses had such lookouts to keep a watch for Indians."

"I've heard and read about them, but this is the first time I've ever seen an Indian peephole," said Brian excitedly.

"Oh, I must climb up there," exclaimed Susan, rushing over to the ladder. "Come, help me lean it against the wall."

"Susan, you could fall!" cried Marge. "It's so high up!"

"The wood might be all rotted by now, if that's the original ladder," added Brian practically.

Heedless of these admonitions, Susan Sand had partially raised the ladder from the floor and, with the assistance of her friends, rested it against the brick wall.

"The bottom rung appears to be sound," she said, placing a foot on the wooden bar. "If the whole thing collapses, Professor Scott and Brian can catch me."

Handing the flashlight to Randall Scott, Susan slowly began ascending toward the Indian peephole. The ladder creaked and tilted precariously to one side as it bore her weight, but the young sleuth kept on until her eyes were level with the tiny rectangular opening.

"How far away the campus seems," she called back to her friends, who stood on the floor below, faithfully trying to hold the ladder steady. "But I don't see any Indians."

Suddenly the girl's body became rigid as she stood on the top rung and gazed through the peephole.

"There is a man down there crouching behind a bush," she breathlessly informed her friends. "He's looking up at this room!"

"Who is it?" three voices asked at once.

"Why, it's the hunched-over man in the trench-coat!" exclaimed Susan.

No sooner had she uttered these portentous words when there was a flutter of wings and a loud squeak from the ceiling above her. A huge bat, disturbed from its roost, rushed past her head, brushing one wing against her face.

Emitting a shriek, Susan tried to grasp the edge of the opening as the ladder lurched away from the peephole, threatening to precipitate her to the floor below.

## Chapter X

## *What the Tory Left Behind*

SUSAN SAND clung frantically to the top of the ladder and leaned her body forward in an attempt to sway herself toward the wall. Stretching out her right hand, she touched the edge of the peephole with the tips of her fingers and then inched them forward, trying to get a firm hold. The bat flapped about the attic room, while Marge screamed in terror and ran toward the stairs.

Professor Scott, fully cognizant of Susan's peril, tried to steady the ladder and assist the girl in directing it against the wall. Brian Lorenzo, aided by his height, flung his jacket at the creature in wide sweeps until he finally managed to maneuver it out one of the windows.

"I've got hold of the edge of the peephole," called Susan with relief. "My, that was a close call!"

"Please come down right away, Sue," pleaded Randall Scott, his face drained of color. "There might be more bats in that nest to startle you."

"Wait just a minute," Susan replied. "I think I've

discovered something. One of these bricks loosened when I grabbed the wall."

"What happened to the man in the trenchcoat?" called Brian.

"He's gone," Susan answered, peering through the small lookout. "He must have heard the commotion."

"Come on down, Sue," begged Randall Scott in a more commanding tone. "You're playing a dangerous game."

"Oh, but I've found something!" she cried elatedly. "This brick comes out, and there is a long, narrow opening in one side of the peephole. There's something in here. A letter! And an earring!"

After thrusting her discovery into the pocket of her skirt and replacing the brick, Susan cautiously descended the ladder. With evident relief, Professor Scott assisted her down the last few rungs.

"Sue, I'm sorry I got so frightened," Marge apologized sheepishly. "I shouldn't have run and screamed like that."

"Nonsense, Marge," replied Susan lightly. "The bat startled me, too. But look what I found!"

As Randall Scott directed the flashlight beam on her hand, Susan reached into her pocket and drew out a letter on yellowed paper. On the folded-over flap was a seal of red wax, and dangling from the seal, obviously stuck fast to the hardened wax, was a magnificent diamond earring!

"Why, it's huge! And it looks like a real diamond!" exclaimed Marge, gazing at the sparkling pendant. "But why is it stuck into that wax seal?"

"The wax must still have been soft when the earring came into contact with the seal," deduced Susan, while the group stared, enthralled, at her discovery. "Think how old this letter must be! And look at the seal!"

"A bird perched on a crown!" Randall Scott cried. "Just like the stained-glass window!"

"And the tattoo!" added Susan.

"What could it all mean?" Brian queried, his face blank with amazement. "Why were they hidden up by that Indian peephole?"

"There is a great significance in all of this," Professor Scott stated solemnly. "I'm beginning to wonder if the mysterious intruder is after this diamond."

"You mean you think he knows about the earring?" asked Marge.

"Yes, I suspect he must know of its existence," he answered.

"But not the exact hiding place! He might still be lurking outside this building," reasoned Susan.

"Let's look at the letter," said Brian impatiently.

Randall Scott pulled a penknife from his pocket and gently inserted the point under the edge of the wax seal.

"Judging from the age of this paper, the author of the letter has been dead for a couple of centuries," he stated with authority.

"And we're the first people ever to read it!" exclaimed Susan. "The seal has never been broken."

Deftly separating the aged wax from the parchment, Professor Scott opened the single piece of thick paper without damaging the seal. The sparkling earring remained fastened into one side of the coin-sized piece of wax.

"The date is May 12, 1775!" cried Marge as Professor Scott illuminated the page with the flashlight.

"Just two days after the British Army lost Fort Ticonderoga to the forces of Ethan Allen," Randall Scott interjected, quickly scanning the old-fashioned handwriting. "Why, the writer of this letter was a Tory named Nathaniel Crowden! He was fleeing to Venezuela!"

"The American Revolution had just begun, and Nathaniel Crowden was on the side of the British. How fascinating!" added Susan. "Professor Scott, do you think the writer of this letter could be an ancestor of Teresa Crowden, Bruce Webb's wife?"

"It certainly does look as if this is the connection we've been seeking," he answered. "According to the letter, Nathaniel Crowden was not only a Tory, opposed to the American Revolution, he was also a jewel thief escaping with his loot."

"Then he must have lived in this house, and the hiding place by the Indian peephole was where he kept his stolen jewels," Susan stated. "He must have scooped up whatever other jewelry was in there in such feverish haste to escape that when he thrust in the letter, the lone earring stuck in the soft wax."

"I don't understand what the letter was doing in the hiding place," Marge said in a puzzled voice.

Randall Scott carefully studied the document. "Apparently Crowden was writing to a confederate by

the name of Luther, informing him that he was fleeing by boat to Caracas, Venezuela. He never had a chance to address the letter. He climbed the ladder, scooped up his stolen jewels from the hiding place, threw in the letter because he didn't want his destination known, and replaced the brick."

"So he was in such a dreadful hurry he didn't realize he had left one earring behind," surmised Marge.

"He couldn't even take time to send the letter or to burn it," added Brian. "Rather than having it discovered on him if he was caught, he threw it in his hiding place."

'Where it has remained with the earring for two hundred years!" Susan said wonderingly.

"Whatever made you pull out the brick, Sue?" Marge asked.

"It was involuntary," the raven-haired girl responded, laughing. "The brick loosened when I grabbed the edge of the peephole trying to save myself from falling. I could see the mortar was crumbling, so I removed the brick and reached in and found the letter."

"Just as simple as that," Professor Scott stated, a note of admiration in his voice. "Most people in your predicament would never have taken such a chance."

"And with a bat flying around!" cried Marge.

"I really didn't have a chance to think," Susan replied, embarrassed by the praise of her friends. "Anyone would have done the same thing."

"What do you intend to do about this valuable earring?" Brian asked, turning to Professor Scott. "Who does it belong to now?"

"Since it was found on university property, I suppose the jewel and the letter belong to Irongate," he replied, holding up the glittering gem. "The letter can go into our archives in Van Delft Library, once we've finished with it. Let's go down to my office and telephone the president of the university. I'll feel better once the diamond is appraised and locked in a safe."

"Yes, if that man in the trenchcoat is after the diamond, he might still be lurking around the grounds," Susan reasoned. "But what about the wax seal? We don't want to damage it by removing the earring."

"For the present it's better to lock both the earring and the letter up together," replied Professor Scott.

With Randall Scott leading the way, the four of them started toward the attic door. At the last minute Brian remembered the open windows.

"We'd better close them in case of rain," he said, striding across the room. "We don't want the attic flooded."

"They'll probably be hard to shut," Marge answered, following him. "I'll give you a hand."

Professor Scott and Susan were already descending the dark stairs and did not realize that Brian and Marge were not behind them.

"Watch your step," called the professor, shining the beam down the stairway. "And keep your head down, Brian."

Slowly Randall Scott and Susan Sand crept down the steep, narrow staircase. Since there were no banisters and scarcely any light, Susan placed a hand on either wall in order to keep her balance and riveted her eyes on her feet to prevent herself from tripping.

Had she not been watching the steps so carefully, she would have seen what was about to happen. Just as Randall Scott opened the bottom door and stepped through, a hand, grasping a weapon, reached out from behind the door and struck him a heavy blow on the head. The flashlight clattered to the floor, and the professor crumpled up in a heap beside it.

While Susan stood momentarily stunned, she saw the hand grab the earring, heard a loud rip, and the arm disappeared. By the time the shocked girl reached Randall Scott's side, the thief was gone and the letter lay on the floor, a jagged tear where the earring and the wax seal had been.

## Chapter XI

### *Held a Prisoner?*

"PROFESSOR SCOTT!" cried Susan Sand, running down the remaining steps without any thought for her own safety. By the time she had reached his side, the young man was stirring, although his color was ashen. The thief was nowhere in sight, but at the end of the hall a swinging door was still moving slightly.

"Oh, what happened?" exclaimed Marge as she and Brian arrived at the bottom of the stairs.

Quickly Susan described the attack and the theft.

"I'll see if I can catch sight of him," said Brian, racing down the corridor and through the swinging doors.

"Be careful, Brian," cautioned Marge. "He might have a gun!"

Susan had managed to assist Randall Scott to a sitting position. "I might as well still be playing football," he said with a rueful smile. "My head feels three sizes too big."

"Someone hit you with a club and stole the earring," Susan explained as Professor Scott rubbed the back of his head. "He could easily have killed you."

"Did you see who he was?" asked Marge, returning from the water cooler with a dampened handkerchief, which she applied to the professor's wound.

"He got me before I even knew there was anyone behind the door," Professor Scott answered. "Did you see him, Sue?"

"Just his hand," replied Susan regretfully. "It was too dark to see anything else. However, I'm almost certain that there is only one person he could be."

Marge studied Susan's thoughtful face as the two girls helped Randall Scott to stand.

"You think he was the hunched-over man in the trenchcoat, don't you, Sue?" she asked.

"It all fits together," Susan answered. "When he struck the blow, I couldn't see the tattoo because the back of his hand was toward me, and it might not have been that wrist that the tattoo is on anyway, but I'm still certain he was the same man. While I was on the ladder, he was lurking outside. He must have entered the building and been waiting for us to come down from the attic."

"Then our theory about the intruder knowing of the existence of the diamond has been proven correct," Randall Scott stated in a professorial tone. "And now *he* has the diamond."

"And the wax seal," added Susan, holding up the parchment letter. Where the seal and the earring had been, there was a jagged tear.

"Maybe we should go to the police," suggested Marge as Brian came running down the hall.

"He's gone!" he said, panting. "I didn't see him, but someone drove off in an old, battered blue car."

"Then he is the same man!" exclaimed Susan. "Remember that old blue car, Marge, that the mysterious intruder drove away from your bookstore?"

"Oh, let's go to the police," Marge repeated.

"Now wait a minute, Marge," said Professor Scott. "Don't be hasty about this. Come into my office, where we can talk it over."

"You can rest there, too, until you're more steady on your feet," Susan said, taking his arm solicitously.

As the group walked toward the office, Susan suddenly stopped short. "Look, there's the seal, lying under that bench!" she cried.

"Yes, it is the seal," said Brian, rushing over and picking up the object.

"It must have loosened when the thief grabbed the earring," Susan surmised. "Then, when he ran with the diamond, the seal fell off."

"At least we recovered something," Professor Scott said, laughing. "The wax can be resealed to the letter, and this historical document will be almost in its original condition."

Once seated behind his desk, Professor Scott stared solemnly at the yellow parchment letter as it lay on the blotter before him, the wax seal beside it.

"Obviously this seal and the stained-glass window bear the coat of arms of Nathaniel Crowden," Randall Scott mused.

"And the tattoo on the intruder's arm is exactly the same as the coat of arms," Susan added. "So maybe the mysterious intruder is a Crowden, like Bruce Webb's wife, Teresa."

"That does make sense," Professor Scott agreed. "There is much more to this than I had first thought. I don't think we should contact the police yet. After all, the earring and the letter have lain in that hiding place, put there by a thief, for two hundred years. I'd rather we looked into the matter for ourselves."

"I agree with you, Professor Scott," replied Susan elatedly. "I know I can solve this mystery and recover the diamond, but I must have time!"

"How can you solve it, Sue?" Marge asked incredulously. "You have no idea where the thief lives, and now we know he's dangerous."

"Nevertheless, I intend to solve it!" Susan emphatically stated. "But right now we must get Professor Scott home."

Vigorously protesting that he felt no ill effects from the blow to his head, Randall Scott was escorted to Susan's car by his three companions and driven to his home. After insisting that he did not need a doctor and promising that he would rest all afternoon, the young man lay down on his couch to study the valuable letter, and the trio left.

Susan drove Marge and Brian to the bookstore and then returned home, where she found Michael Leeds waiting for her in the living room.

"I just had to see you, Miss Sand," he said, his face flushed with excitement and his hands nervously fidgeting with his cloth cap.

"Sit down, Mr. Leeds," said Susan comfortingly. "What has happened?"

"I've been fired."

"Fired! Oh dear," she moaned. "Bruce Webb must have seen us talking. I'm sorry, Mr. Leeds. It's all my fault."

"No, Miss Sand. I'm sure it's not that. He's hired another gardener."

"Another gardener? But he just hired you. He must still be angry about our talking."

"No, that's not the reason," Michael Leeds insisted. "He seems to know this new fellow. There is something queer about the way he treats him."

"Really?" said Susan, sitting on the edge of the couch and adjusting her glasses. "How very interesting. How does he treat him?"

"Like he's afraid of him."

"When did you notice this?"

"Well, when I got to work this morning I started for the tool shed to get the clipping shears. The bushes along the driveway needed cutting badly. I no sooner got to the shed when Webb comes running out of the house, followed by this fellow. I didn't like this new fellow's looks."

"What did he look like?"

"Hunched over and kind of mean."

"Was he wearing a trenchcoat?" Susan asked, trying to hide her excitement.

"Yes, as a matter of fact he was. Why do you ask that?"

"I just thought I might be able to recognize him if I saw him," Susan answered evasively, not wanting to reveal too much to the gardener. "But what happened to make you think that Bruce Webb was afraid of this new gardener?"

"Because I heard the fellow say to Webb, 'I'll live here if I want to, and you can't stop me.' I know I wasn't supposed to hear what he said, but I did."

"And then Bruce Webb made up a story about hiring this man to replace you?" Susan said significantly.

"That's how I see it. He said I wasn't doing my work fast enough and that he needed a younger man."

"I'm certain that was just his excuse to fire you," Susan replied gently. "Did Bruce Webb seem very angry when he fired you?"

"No. That's the funny part of it. He kept looking back at this man standing on the porch. It was like I wasn't even there."

"Did the man in the trenchcoat say anything else to Bruce Webb?"

"No. He just kept standing on the porch, sort of glaring at him. I wouldn't want to be mixed up with that fellow."

"Thank you very much, Mr. Leeds, for telling me this. I'm sure that you will be able to find another job, and a much safer one," Susan assured him.

"It's just as well that it happened, now that I've had a chance to think about it," said the gardener, pulling on his cloth cap. "Whatever they're doing in that house, I don't want to be involved in it. If I was Mrs. Manning, I'd get out of there fast."

"I think you are right," Susan adamantly replied.

"Mrs. Manning should not be working at Hollowhearth House."

Before Michael Leeds left Susan's house, the young author presented him with a copy of *The Bony Finger*, which she inscribed: "To Michael Leeds in gratitude for all his help." The gardener was so overcome with emotion that Susan promised him she would make certain he received a copy of her next book as soon as it was published.

"The hunched-over man in the trenchcoat is living at Hollowhearth House," Susan said out loud as soon as the gardener had left. "He has some sort of hold over Bruce Webb. I'll call Professor Scott immediately!"

Randall Scott was astounded by the information Susan had to relate.

"So Bruce is involved with the thief!" he said over the wire.

"And he is afraid of him," added Susan. "Oh, I must phone Mrs. Manning this minute!"

"I think you should, Sue. I'd like to come over and talk to you about this, but my car is still at the university."

"No, Professor Scott, you must rest. I'll contact Mrs. Manning and then come over to your house."

"There's one thing I've remembered, lying here on the couch," the young professor said before Susan could hang up the telephone. "About five years ago there was a break-in at Piper Hall. I was still a student at that time, but I remember that all the rooms were turned topsy-turvy, yet nothing was stolen. Everyone thought it was very strange."

"Then you think the thief was looking for the diamond that long ago?"

"Yes, I do. He must be a Crowden, and he would undoubtedly know that his ancestor, Nathaniel Crowden, lived in the house when it was a private home and before the Piper family owned it."

"That does make sense!" exclaimed Susan. "But where is the other earring?"

"Now you are complicating matters." Randall Scott chuckled. "One diamond earring is enough to think about."

"Well, I'm going to concentrate on two earrings," Susan playfully replied as she bade the young man good-bye.

She immediately telephoned Mrs. Manning. The cook said that she was anxious to see Susan, for she too had something important to relate.

Within ten minutes the young girl was seated in Mrs. Manning's living room, telling the woman of the discovery and theft at the university and the gardener's description of the man in the trenchcoat.

"I'm not surprised at anything you've told me," Mrs. Manning replied when Susan had finished. "I haven't seen the new gardener, but this morning Bruce Webb called me to come and fix breakfast. When I was in the kitchen making coffee and frying bacon, a very queer thing happened. Somehow I felt like I wasn't alone. I turned around, and there, standing in the doorway, was a young woman. She looked terrified."

"A woman!" Susan cried. "Maybe she's Teresa Crowden, Bruce Webb's wife!"

"I don't know who she is, but when I spoke to her,

Bruce Webb suddenly appeared in the shadows. 'I told you to stay in your room,' he said to her in a whisper. Then he grabbed her arm and pulled her away from the door."

"What did she look like?" Susan asked, her green eyes widening.

"She was very pretty, with an olive complexion, jet-black hair, and dark, sad eyes," Mrs. Manning replied.

"She sounds as if she could be South American!" Susan exclaimed. "She must be Teresa Crowden."

"He didn't call her by name. I'm sure the poor thing wanted to talk to me."

"Oh, Mrs. Manning, we must get inside that house! Teresa Crowden might be in danger!"

"I don't know how you're going to manage that, Susan," the cook answered, shaking her head. "Sounds awful dangerous to me. I'm not going back there again."

"No, you mustn't," Susan emphatically agreed, tossing her black hair over her shoulders.

Susan questioned Mrs. Manning further but could elicit nothing more from the frightened woman. After promising the cook that she would be careful, Susan departed, a daring thought forming in her mind.

"I'll go to Hollowhearth House tonight!" she murmured to herself. "No one will see me in the dark if I hide in the bushes under the windows. I'll find out if Teresa Crowden is being held a prisoner!"

## Chapter XII

## *Midnight on Hollowhearth Hill*

"I'LL go to Hollowhearth House tonight!" Susan Sand repeated to herself. "But this time I won't be seen!"

With this daring plan racing through her brain, Susan drove back to Thornewood. Before visiting Professor Scott she decided to stop at Marge's bookstore and bring her friend up to date on the fast-moving events.

Susan found Marge arranging books on a shelf in one corner of the shop. As soon as she saw her good friend's troubled expression, she felt a wave of sympathy for her, and then a flood of anger toward Bruce Webb, who had caused Marge so much unhappiness.

In response to Susan's cheerful greeting, Marge Halloran barely managed a smile. Rushing over from the corner, she pulled a piece of paper from her purse and thrust it into Susan's hand.

"I found this on the seat of my car this afternoon," she said in a quavering voice. "Susan, what could it mean? I'm getting more frightened all the time."

"A drawing of a black bird perched on a crown!" gasped Susan, gazing at the crude sketch on the paper. "The Crowden coat of arms!"

Underneath the drawing was the single word BEWARE in bold hand-lettering.

"Someone put it in my car this afternoon, Sue," repeated Marge. "Brian and I found it when you dropped us off. What are we going to do?"

"First of all, I don't want you to get upset," replied Susan firmly. "The only purpose of this message is to scare you away from Hollowhearth House."

"Oh, Sue, what would I do without you? You can always manage to keep your head. I wish I could say the same for myself."

Trying to gather herself together, Marge went behind the counter to wait on a customer. Susan stood staring at the eerie symbol in her hand.

"This is most likely the work of our lurking thief," she thought. "He probably learned from Bruce Webb that Marge should really own Hollowhearth. Now he's trying to break her down."

"Sue," whispered Marge after the customer had left, "maybe we should call the police."

Susan shook her head. "Not yet," she replied quietly. "We have no way of proving who left this paper, any more than we have of who stole the earring. Professor Scott and I agreed that for now we'll do our own investigating."

"I suppose you are right, as usual," sighed Marge. "What do you propose to do?"

"I have a plan," replied Susan guardedly. "I've just visited Mrs. Manning, and she told me a very queer tale."

While Marge listened with rapt attention, Susan briefly related the story of the dark-eyed woman at Hollowhearth House.

"How dreadful!" exclaimed her friend. "What can we do except call the police?"

"I'm going to Professor Scott's to talk it over with him," Susan responded. "And I'll show him this threatening piece of paper."

"Sue, what are you scheming?" Marge asked suspiciously. "You said you had a plan."

"If I tell you, you'll only worry," replied her friend. "Just leave everything to me."

With a final encouraging word to Marge, Susan Sand started for Randall Scott's home, the menacing note in her purse. The young man's housekeeper admitted the girl and showed her into the living room.

"I'm glad to see you so soon," said the professor cheerfully, rising from his easy chair. "What news have you brought now?"

"I had to show you this," Susan said, placing the paper in his hand. "Marge found it on the seat of her car this afternoon."

Randall Scott whistled softly as he studied the paper. "They're getting somewhat desperate, don't you think, Sue?" he said presently.

"Is that how you interpret it?"

"Certainly. If they weren't frightened, they wouldn't have to resort to scare tactics."

"That's my opinion exactly," she agreed. "I wondered if you would think the same way."

"And now that you know I do, what are you planning as your next move?"

Susan smiled and replaced the crude threat in her purse. "You seem to be able to read my mind," she replied quietly.

"Just don't do anything foolish," he cautioned. "I can see that you have something up your sleeve."

"My next move is a necessary one," she answered cryptically.

Randall Scott escorted Susan to the door and stood looking after her with a worried expression on his handsome face.

"Please be careful, Sue," he called as she hurried to her car. "I wish you would tell me what you are plotting."

Susan shook her head and waved good-bye as she drove away from the curb. So vital was her trip to Hollowhearth that she had decided against telling anyone, lest someone try to prevent her from going through with the plan.

Later that evening, after a delicious dinner cooked by Mrs. Draper, Susan prepared for the night's adventure. After changing her clothes and making certain she had her flashlight, the young girl went down to Professor Sand's study, but her aunt was so engrossed in her university work that Susan decided not to disturb her.

As the courageous sleuth backed her car from the driveway, the rain that had threatened all day burst forth in a torrent.

"Of all the luck," thought Susan ruefully. "I hope this doesn't keep up for long. The cliff road will be nothing but mud."

There was little traffic during the trip to Hollowhearth Hill, and Susan Sand soon arrived at the turnoff. The winding private road that led up the hill was muddy and dotted with small pools of water.

"With such poor visibility I have less chance of being seen," she said to herself, parking in the same secluded spot she had used when she spoke with Michael Leeds.

Attired in black knee-high boots and black raincoat and hat, Susan climbed out of her car into the wet night. Her flashlight securely in her hand, she started cautiously up the hill, staying well to the side of the road. A brisk wind blew the rain in her face and whined through the thick trees. Above her, in the windows of the old house, a few lights flickered.

"I suppose I should be grateful for the foul weather," she murmured, pulling her raincoat closely around her. "No one can see through this deluge."

Susan decided that the most advantageous place to begin her sleuthing was by the dining-room window. In order to reach that wing of the big house, she had to cross the road toward the driveway. Glancing at the structure and seeing no one, she dashed across the road to the other side and flattened herself against a broad tree trunk. For minutes she did not move. There was no sound but the rain and wind.

"Safe!" she thought and crept swiftly through the trees in the direction of the dining room.

Susan resolved to take up her post in a cluster of shrubbery near one of the large windows and wait for the lights to be extinguished. Overhead the branches of a big oak tree afforded some protection, but the wind continued and the girl was pelted by the blowing rain. In order to see at all, she had to remove her glasses constantly and wipe them on a handkerchief.

The wait seemed endless. Several times she carefully rose above the window ledge and peered into the dining room. It was empty. Once she made a tour of the house but could see nothing in any of the chambers. Afraid of giving herself away if she should attempt to spy through the lighted windows, Susan returned to her hiding place.

Two hours passed, and by midnight the wind had lessened but the rain continued unabated. The lights in the front windows were barely visible, but Susan could still see them glowing eerily through the haze. No one had appeared. Refusing to despair, she crouched patiently behind the bushes. Suddenly the porch light went on! At the same time the other lights were extinguished and figures emerged through the front door.

"Three people!" gasped Susan.

As the trio came toward the driveway, the girl crouched lower and parted the shrubbery in order to get a good look at her quarry. One of the three was a woman! The man with Bruce Webb was definitely the hunched-over man in the trenchcoat. He was carrying a small package, which was wrapped in brown paper.

Bruce Webb headed for the garage and opened the doors, but the woman and the other man hung back. They appeared to be having an argument.

"I see no reason why I have to go with you," cried the woman.

"Because I say you do, Teresa," said the man, grasping her arm in a viselike grip. "The trip will take only a couple of hours."

"Teresa!" said Susan softly to herself. "Teresa Crowden, Bruce Webb's wife!"

Reluctantly the woman followed the man to the garage. They passed within ten feet of Susan. The expression on the woman's face was one of anger mixed with fear. Even Bruce Webb seemed subdued by the stranger, for he said nothing as the group got into the car.

"I must follow them! But how can I get back to my car in time?" Susan was frantic for fear she would lose track of them if they had too much of a head start. Then she decided on a desperate move. Chancing that no one would turn around once they were in the car, Susan dashed from her hiding place, crossed the driveway, and headed for the seclusion of the hedges on the other side.

Breathlessly she threw herself on the soaking ground in the middle of a grove of birch trees. Her glasses flew off and landed several feet away. For several moments she lay still as the yellow convertible backed down the driveway, turned around in a clearing, and started down the road.

Susan realized that she would have to wait for the convertible to pass her before she could get to her car.

As soon as she felt it was a safe distance away, she retrieved her glasses, ran to her car, and followed the red taillights to the highway.

The yellow car turned west, the opposite direction from Thornewood. Because the traffic was light at such a late hour, Susan was especially careful not to get too close. For half an hour the convertible remained on the highway, then veered suddenly off to the right onto a narrow two-lane road.

After another two miles, the car slowed down abruptly and stopped in front of a small dilapidated cottage. Keeping a good distance away, Susan stopped also. Jumping out of her car and moving nearer to the bungalow, she watched as the three of them mounted the wooden steps and knocked on the door.

The rain was still falling, but not as heavily. Because of the haze, seeing any great distance was difficult. As the door opened, Susan strained to catch a glimpse of the person who stood in the doorway, but she was too far away to make out the figure. When the three of them had gone inside and the door closed, Susan moved nearer to the structure. As she did so, a light went on in the basement.

"I must see what they are doing!" she murmured and crept over to look through the cellar window.

## Chapter XIII

# *Spying*

SUSAN SAND crept silently to one side of the cellar window and peered around the edge of the cement foundation. She had an excellent view of the basement of the shabby cottage. A bare bulb hanging from the ceiling shed a glaring light through the small room. Except for a plain wooden table and several chairs in one corner, there was no furniture. Opposite the stairway was a closed door, fastened with a heavy metal padlock.

As Susan cautiously looked through the dirty window, she was able to study the person who had admitted the trio—a tall woman of middle age, so nicely dressed that she seemed out of place in her surroundings.

While the four people stood in the center of the little room, Susan noticed that the hunched-over man, who seemed to have some hold over Bruce Webb and the woman called Teresa, still held in his hand the small package she had seen earlier.

As Bruce Webb talked to the elegantly dressed

woman, he reached out his hand to take the package from his companion. Susan drew in a breath when she saw his bared arm. The bandage was gone, and on his wrist was the same bird tattoo!

The hunched-over man stepped back and refused to yield the parcel. Instead, he started to undo the string, while Bruce Webb, his brow creased in anger, stood to one side, watching.

"He certainly acts as if he is the boss," observed Susan. "Bruce Webb has hardly said two words."

Before the man had the package open, the owner of the cottage said something to him and motioned to the locked door. Walking over to it, she drew a key from her pocket and undid the lock. In a moment the four of them had disappeared into the next room.

"What rotten luck," said Susan ruefully as she waited for the group to reappear. "Now I'll never be able to see what's in that package."

Minutes went by while Susan impatiently remained by the window. The rain had almost stopped, but she was chilled to the bone from the gusting wind. Glancing at her watch, she saw that it was almost one-thirty.

"Oh, I do wish they would hurry," she moaned. "Aunt Adele will have the entire police force out looking for me if I'm not home soon."

Still the quartet did not appear, but Susan remained tenaciously by the window. Several moments later the door swung open, and Teresa reentered the room. Her dark eyes revealed even more fear than they had earlier. As she covertly looked at the cellar stairs and then back over her shoulder, she seemed to be trying to come to a decision.

"I think she wants to run away," surmised Susan. "What could they be doing in that room to make her so frightened?"

Suddenly, without warning, Teresa looked up at the window and saw Susan. The young sleuth momentarily drew back, but something in the woman's eyes made her stop, for Teresa seemed to be glad to see her. There was a pleading expression in those dark eyes, as if she was asking for help.

Before Susan could think of what to do, the tall woman emerged from the other room, followed by Bruce Webb and the hunched-over man. The package was still firmly in the latter's hand, rewrapped and tied securely. Saying what seemed to be some harsh words to Teresa, he grabbed her arm and pulled her roughly to the stairway. The door was relocked, the light was extinguished, and the group mounted to thc ground floor.

"Well, my night trip was worth the effort," thought Susan. "Teresa was actually begging me to help her escape!"

Within moments the trio left the cottage and drove off in the yellow convertible. Susan thought that to pursue them any longer would be a waste of time. "They'll probably go right back to Hollowhearth," she reasoned, "and with Teresa as their prisoner."

Susan started back to her car, but abruptly stopped in her tracks. Another daring plan had begun to form in her mind. Who was the tall, nicely dressed woman, and what was in the package? Perhaps there was a way of finding out the answer to at least one of the questions.

Continuing on, she arrived at her car, got in, and waited for about ten minutes. Then she started the motor, drove onto the road, and pulled up in front of the shabby cottage. Jumping out, she walked rapidly to the door and knocked loudly. In a moment the door opened and the tall woman stood in the dim light.

"I'm very sorry to bother you at such a late hour, but I saw your lights on," began Susan. "Would you mind if I used your telephone?"

Hesitating for several seconds, the woman said nothing. She seemed undecided about admitting a stranger so late at night.

"You see, I took a wrong turn and went miles out of my way," continued Susan, quickly inventing an explanation for her presence in the neighborhood. "My aunt will be absolutely frantic."

"Come in," the woman replied. "The phone is in the hall."

Susan smiled her most charming smile and stepped into the dingy room. She found it difficult to believe that this woman lived in the house, for what furniture there was appeared old and dilapidated. The floors were thick with dust, and the curtains hung in filthy rags on the windows.

As Susan crossed the hall to the telephone and picked up the receiver, she noticed a little red book lying on the table next to the instrument. Moving to her left so that her body concealed her actions, she opened the book to the first page. There, on the inside cover, was a name and address:

Barbara Lauder
723 Creighton Drive
Crescent City

Susan imprinted the name and address firmly in her mind. Quickly dialing her own number, she soon heard Professor Sand's voice.

"Susan! Where have you been?" cried her aunt. "Mrs. Draper and I were going to call the police. I just phoned Professor Scott to see if he knew where you were."

"I'm all right, Aunt Adele," replied Susan soothingly. "I took a wrong turn. I'm in a little cottage about twenty miles from Thornewood. The woman who lives here has graciously let me use her phone. I should be home in about half an hour."

The tall woman watched Susan Sand as she talked to her aunt. Had she seen her open the red book? Susan thought not, for the woman had a blank expression on her face and seemed preoccupied.

After bidding her aunt good-bye and thanking her benefactor, Susan left the cottage and headed for Thornewood. "I hope I didn't make a mistake," she thought. "Now Barbara Lauder knows what I look like. But at least I did find out her name. I wonder how she could be mixed up with Bruce Webb and the hunched-over man? And what reason could there be for using that cellar room?"

At two-fifteen in the morning Susan Sand pulled into the driveway of her home. Parked in front of the house was Randall Scott's automobile.

"Oh my, I certainly have worried everyone," said Susan guiltily to herself. "But wait until they hear about my adventure!"

Once the greetings were over, Susan, her aunt, the young professor, and the housekeeper seated themselves around the table in the spacious dining room to listen to Susan's story and enjoy an early-morning snack which Mrs. Draper had quickly prepared.

"I had no idea you were planning such a bold move, Sue," said Randall Scott, sipping his coffee. "If I had known, I would have insisted on accompanying you."

"I thought you would try to stop me, and it was vital that I find out if Teresa Crowden was really a prisoner in Hollowhearth House," Susan replied earnestly. "I was fortunate that I went there on a night when Bruce Webb made one of the trips that Michael Leeds told me about."

"And you really think that the woman is Teresa Crowden and that she is a prisoner of those two men?" Professor Sand asked. "Why would a man keep his own wife prisoner?"

"She must know something," Susan replied emphatically. "She is very frightened. When she saw me looking through the cellar window, instead of giving me away, she appealed to me for help. I could tell by her pleading expression."

"But why is Bruce Webb afraid of the other man?" Randall Scott wondered out loud.

"I don't know. But I did discover that Bruce Webb has the same tattoo on his arm. The bandage was gone, and there was no question that it was that same mark."

"It must be some sort of gang," mused the young man. "And the hunched-over man is the boss. But why did they go to the cottage with that brown package?"

"My guess is that Barbara Lauder met them there to look at the contents of the package," Susan answered, tossing back her shiny black hair.

"Barbara Lauder!" Mrs. Draper exclaimed, abruptly setting down her coffee cup. "She owns a jewelry store in Crescent City. She is a very respectable citizen."

"A jewelry store!" cried Susan in amazement. "Don't you see what that must mean? Barbara Lauder is a dealer in stolen gems!"

## Chapter XIV

## *Dr. Endicott's Story*

"THE DIAMOND earring must have been in that brown package!" Susan Sand declared.

"Then Barbara Lauder is a fence," reasoned Randall Scott. "And after the hunched-over man stole the earring from us, he went to Bruce Webb. Together they are attempting to sell it through Barbara Lauder."

"That has to be the answer to their meeting at the shabby cottage," Susan mused. "But why would the hunched-over man take Bruce Webb into his confidence?"

"As Professor Scott said, they must be members of a gang," Aunt Adele concluded.

"The tattoos indicate that," Susan agreed. "But I still think there is a great deal to the mystery that we don't know."

By the time Randall Scott departed, all further speculation on the Hollowhearth House mystery had been thoroughly exhausted and every possible theory advanced. Susan retired to bed immediately and slept late into Sunday morning.

All that day the rain continued, and the young girl spent most of the dreary hours analyzing every detail of the problem. She tried to work on her next book, but her mind refused to concentrate. Marge had called right after breakfast, and Susan related the happenings of the previous night to her astonished friend.

Not until Sunday evening did anything of importance occur, when Professor Scott telephoned to say that Dr. Endicott had returned from Venezuela.

"Professor Endicott is back already!" exclaimed Susan. "He said in his cable that he wouldn't return for several days."

"He arrived about eight o'clock this evening. We had a chance to do some talking before he retired."

"What does he have to say?" asked Susan impatiently.

"A great deal. The Crowdens are notorious. They have terrorized the entire area around Caracas. They are involved in every kind of crime—kidnapping, blackmail, government intrigue . . ."

"How dreadful!" cried Susan. "Is that why he found it necessary to come back from such important research instead of writing to us?"

"I'd rather not discuss the matter over the phone," replied the young man guardedly.

"You mean it's too serious?" asked Susan with deepening interest.

"Yes. Dr. Endicott thinks he might have been followed from South America. He was afraid to return to his own home. That's why he's staying with me."

"What!" cried Susan.

"He took an earlier flight in order to avoid being detected. He doesn't know whether he escaped them or not."

"Them?"

"Two men, as far as he knows. I haven't heard half of what he has to say because he was too tired to tell me the entire story. He's sleeping now. Come over around ten o'clock tomorrow morning with Marge and Brian, and you can hear the rest of his adventure."

After thanking Professor Scott and assuring him that she would see him in the morning, Susan prepared for bed. Her mind was a confusion of unanswered questions, yet, despite her mental turmoil, she slept soundly until Icky plumped on her bed the next morning and patted her face with one soft paw.

Susan's first thought upon awakening was of Teresa Crowden.

"Ikhnaton, do you think that Teresa told those two men that she saw me in the cellar window?"

Icky purred loudly as Susan drew him into her arms and hugged him tightly.

"That question must have been preying on my subconscious mind," she told herself. "I'm sure Teresa wants me to help her escape from them."

Before Susan was halfway through breakfast, Marge arrived, eager to hear the details of her friend's nighttime adventure.

"Dr. Endicott never realized what he was getting into when he agreed to do some investigating for us," Susan said. "I'd feel responsible if something should happen to him because of me. Maybe the time has come to call the police."

"I think you should call Chief Burton," said Mrs. Draper vehemently as she buttered a piece of toast for Susan. "I don't like any of it. Why, there's no telling what they are up to, what with following Professor Endicott and running out to that bungalow to see Barbara Lauder."

"We are going over to Professor Scott's right now, Mrs. Draper. I am going to ask him if he thinks Dr. Endicott might need protection," said Susan.

Susan drove first to Brian Lorenzo's house after Marge had telephoned him and asked him to accompany them. During the trip the red-haired girl chattered nervously, while Brian sat quietly, now and then offering some thoughts of his own.

"I've been puzzled from the beginning about what Mr. Leeds described. Remember when he saw Bruce Webb reaching up into the air? Now what do you make of that?" he asked Susan.

"Nothing at all thus far," she replied, "but everything we see and hear must be examined as a possible clue."

Upon arriving at Randall Scott's home, the three friends were ushered into the study by his housekeeper. Dr. Giles Endicott was sitting in a large leather chair, sipping a cup of coffee and talking animatedly to his host.

"Professor Endicott," said Susan to the little man, "I'm sorry to have involved you in all this."

"I wouldn't have missed the experience for the world," he replied elatedly, pulling his goatee. "It makes me feel like Sherlock Holmes."

"Don't you think we should call the police?" said

Susan gently. "Professor Scott told me you might have been followed from Venezuela."

"There were two men trailing me in Caracas," Dr. Endicott replied. "I didn't see them on the plane. If they should appear in Thornewood, that will be time enough to call the police."

"I don't want you endangered," said Susan with concern. "I'm grateful you got back to the United States safely. Now, please tell us what happened when you arrived in Caracas."

"To begin with, everyone I spoke with about the Crowdens was afraid of them. I received your cable within an hour after I arrived at my hotel. Casually, I mentioned the name Crowden to the bellboy. I asked him if he knew where they lived and how I might see them. The boy refused to come to my room after that. He never spoke to me again."

"You mean he was *that* afraid?" asked Susan.

"He was terrified," returned Dr. Endicott.

"Then how did you find out anything?" queried Brian.

"I went to the police. They told me everything they knew. The Crowdens are known locally as the Crow People."

"The Crow People! Then the bird on the coat of arms is a crow!"

"That's correct," responded Dr. Endicott. "Sidney Crowden, Teresa's father, is called the Black Hood and is the power behind the Crow People. His rule is tyrannical, and those who disobey him are dealt with ruthlessly."

"But Bruce Webb has the tattoo on his arm, so that means that they are not all blood relations," stated Susan.

"Yes, they are not. Many people have been inducted into the gang, some willingly, others for fear of their lives. Some, like Webb, married into it." The little man's face was grave. "Anyone who has become a member always has the crow symbol tattooed on the forearm.

"And now," Dr. Endicott continued, smiling broadly, "I have something to relate that is both astonishing and ironic. You, Miss Sand, found the missing Stardrop Earring. The Crowdens have always had possession of one earring. They knew that the other earring had been accidentally left behind by Nathaniel Crowden somewhere in their ancestral home, which, as you know, is now part of Irongate University—called Piper Hall because the Piper family owned it after the Tory Crowdens fled from America."

"The Stardrop Earring," Susan interjected as Dr. Endicott paused.

"That's what the gem is called, Sue," replied Randall Scott. "Bruce Webb stole the other one of the pair from the Crowdens."

"The Caracas police," continued Professor Endicott, "described the earrings as huge diamonds, flawless and perfectly cut. Each one is worth many thousands of dollars. Randall tells me that Nathaniel Crowden, besides being a Tory, was a jewel thief and inadvertently left one earring in that hiding place by the Indian peephole in his haste to flee from America. I understand that the jewel Miss Sand found is very large and beautiful."

"It's magnificent!" said Marge ecstatically. "It is shaped like a pear and is absolutely huge!"

"Do you mean, Dr. Endicott, that Bruce Webb stole the Stardrop Earring from his own wife's family?" asked Brian in shocked surprise.

"That's correct. Webb had planned his escape well ahead. He had already booked passage on *El Cometa*. Then the police seem to have lost the trail. They thought that he was drowned when the ship sank."

"But somehow he managed to get away with the earring," surmised Susan. "No wonder he's afraid!"

"The police abandoned the investigation after the ship disaster," continued the little professor. "Bruce Webb was thought to be dead, and the case was closed."

Susan sat thinking for some time. "Then it's most likely that the Black Hood is suspicious about Bruce Webb's drowning," she said presently. "He has been searching for him ever since the ship sank."

"That makes sense, Miss Sand," Professor Endicott replied. "I think the Black Hood is having every person followed who might lead him to the Stardrop. Members of the Crow People were trailing me because I went to the police. Then they became suspicious of my activities. The Black Hood must have spies all over Caracas."

"I can understand now why the man in the Venezuelan Steamship Office acted the way he did," said Susan. "He knows something about the Crow

People. He didn't want to show me the passenger list until he had seen my wrist and was certain that I wasn't a member."

"There are still many unanswered questions," said Professor Scott. "Why, if she's a Crowden, does Teresa look South American?"

"That's because she is an *adopted* daughter of Sidney Crowden," replied Dr. Endicott. "In all this excitement, I completely forgot to tell you that."

"Oh, she isn't really one of them," said Susan. "And yet she is in their power. We have to free her and find the hiding place of those earrings before they locate a buyer for them!"

"Susan Sand, what are you plotting now?" asked Randall Scott, studying her intently.

"How to get inside Hollowhearth House," she replied.

"Inside Hollowhearth! How could you ever accomplish that?" Professor Scott looked concerned at Susan's bold answer.

"I have ways," responded Susan, with a sly smile. "And no one within Hollowhearth House will be the wiser."

## Chapter XV

## *In Disguise*

"SUSAN SAND, you can't go back to that house now!" cried Marge. "How do you expect to get inside? You'll end up a prisoner yourself."

"Not if I'm in disguise," replied Susan.

"Disguise!" Brian exclaimed.

"Yes. I've had quite a bit of experience in the Thornewood Thespians," Susan continued. "I know something about make-up and costume. I'm certain I could be convincing."

"Even if you fool Bruce Webb and the hunched-over man, what would you expect to accomplish by getting into the house?" asked Randall Scott.

"I might be able to help Teresa," she replied. "And there is the possibility that I could discover where the Stardrops are hidden."

"Miss Sand, the Crow People should be carefully dealt with," warned Dr. Endicott. "Remember that the Black Hood had me followed merely because I asked some questions about the Crowdens."

"Perhaps the time has come to call in the police,"

Professor Scott said thoughtfully. "We know Bruce Webb stole one earring. Why not have him arrested?"

"We don't have the evidence until we find the earrings," countered Susan.

"That is very sound reasoning, Sue," Randall Scott replied. "The evidence to convict the two men is inside Hollowhearth House."

"Unless the earrings have already been disposed of through Barbara Lauder," Brian reminded everyone.

"Nevertheless, I must follow through with my plan and take the chance the earrings are still there," Susan stated decisively.

"What about Teresa?" Marge asked apprehensively. "If she is being held prisoner, you would have to search the entire house to find her."

Susan refused to discuss the matter further until she had time to consider the most appropriate disguise for her entry into Hollowhearth. After she had thanked Dr. Endicott for his invaluable assistance and promised Randall Scott she would inform him when her plan was ready to be carried out, the three young people returned to Susan's house. Immediately Susan excused herself and hurried up the oak staircase to her bedroom, leaving her friends waiting expectantly downstairs. Forty-five minutes later their patience was rewarded.

At the top of the stairway appeared the figure of an elderly woman, somewhat bent over and leaning on a cane. Her pure white hair was braided and wrapped into a neat pile at the back of her head. She was wearing a white blouse trimmed with lace and a long

blue skirt. A hand-knitted shawl was thrown over her shoulders.

"Susan!" cried Marge as the old woman descended the stairs, taking each step cautiously. "Is that really you?"

"I'm sure I don't know who you mean, young lady," came the reply in a high, strident voice. "Who is this young man with you?"

"Well, I'll be . . ." said the astonished Brian. "I would never know you, Susan. It's fantastic!"

The old woman smiled as she slowly sank onto the sofa. "If I can fool my close friends, I can fool Bruce Webb," she replied in her normal voice. "And the hunched-over man as well."

"What are you planning to do, Sue?" asked Marge. "Pose as an old flower lady?"

"No, that would never do." Susan laughed. "I—"

The "old woman" was interrupted by the doorbell.

"It's Randall Scott's car," said Brian, looking out the window. "He's worried about you, Sue. I think he wants to make certain you don't get into trouble."

"This is a good test of your disguise," said Marge on her way to open the door.

Professor Scott greeted Marge and entered the living room. Seeing the old lady, he hesitated, obviously waiting to be introduced.

"Professor Scott, I see you have never met Susan's great-aunt, Mrs. Wexford," said Brian with swift presence of mind.

"How do you do," murmured Randall Scott, bowing politely toward the old woman.

Marge had started to giggle, and Brian had his hand over his mouth, trying to muffle a laugh.

"Where's Susan?" asked the professor, looking about the room. "I've been thinking about that daring plan of hers—"

He stopped abruptly and stared at Marge for a moment and then glanced at Brian. Wrinkling his brow into a frown, he studied the old woman intently.

"It can't be," he murmured in disbelief.

"Oh, but it is," assured Marge. "Isn't she marvelous? I'll bet Professor Sand and Mrs. Draper wouldn't know her either."

"I'm sure they wouldn't," continued Randall Scott. "Susan, you're an artist. I *knew* you were planning on a disguise, yet I still didn't recognize you."

Susan brushed off his praise lightly. "Then I can be certain Bruce Webb would never recognize me," she said. "If my plan works this afternoon, we might be close to finding the Stardrop Earrings."

Susan called a taxi to take her to Hollowhearth House. To go in her own car would certainly give her away, and allowing anyone to accompany her would take an unnecessary chance of being discovered.

An apprehensive group saw Susan off on her journey. Professor Scott was still extremely dubious about the venture, although his attitude had changed somewhat now that he had seen Susan in her disguise.

As she sat in the back of the cab, Susan carefully thought over her plan.

"It just must work," she told herself. "If I can only

remain inside the house long enough to discover something worthwhile."

Once in front of Hollowhearth House, Susan drew in a deep breath and stepped from the cab. As the driver carefully assisted her, she could not help chuckling to herself at his gentle treatment. The cabby promised to wait for her return, if she was not too long.

Slowly Susan climbed the wooden steps and knocked on the door. Minutes passed and no one answered, although somebody had heard her, for the curtains in a front window moved slightly. Then the door swung open, and Bruce Webb stood glumly looking down at her.

"Good afternoon, Mr. Webb," she began in a shrill voice. "I'm so very glad you are at home. You see, I'm from the Thornewood Historical Society, and ever since we learned about the valuable items in this old place, we just—"

"What do you want?" he gruffly interrupted. "I'm in the middle of something. Nothing in the house is for sale."

"But the Historical Society is willing to pay a very high price for some of your precious antiques," replied Susan, smiling.

"A high price? How high?" asked Bruce with sudden interest.

"Now, that depends on the item," answered Susan, stepping into the foyer. "But there are two articles that I am especially interested in."

"How come you know so much about what's in this

house?" Bruce asked in a suspicious tone, searching her with his deep-set eyes.

"Mr. Webb, if you will just help me over to that chair, I will tell you what great treasures you have here."

Susan leaned on her cane and, taking Bruce Webb's arm, started toward a chair. "The Historical Society has been interested in this house for a long time," she continued. "We had a tour through here before you owned it. Look at this beautiful chair," she said, patting the arm lovingly with her gloved hand.

"Yeah, what about it?" returned Bruce Webb.

"Why, there are not many of these chairs left, especially in such good condition," continued Susan, her eyes methodically looking over the large living room.

The room looked very much the same as the day she had been there with Marge and Randall Scott, except for one major difference. The door leading into the hall to the rear wing was closed.

"But I am most interested in two Civil War uniforms," Susan rambled on, sitting down in the antique chair.

"Civil War uniforms?"

"Yes. If I remember correctly, all the clothes are upstairs in the main bedroom," she replied. "Mr. Webb, don't you realize how exciting it is to live in a house surrounded by all this history?" Susan pulled a lace handkerchief from her sleeve and dabbed her face.

"I can't say I'm interested in history," returned

Bruce Webb. "But if you want to buy those uniforms, I'll go get them for you."

"Oh, that would be most kind," she replied quietly. "I would love to go upstairs with you, but I'm afraid the climb is too steep. I'm not so young anymore, you know. I'll just sit here and wait for you."

"How will I know what to look for?" he asked, starting for the staircase.

"They are dark blue, Mr. Webb, with gold buttons," explained Susan. "I'm sure you will find them."

Bruce Webb quickly climbed the stairs and disappeared down the hall. In a flash Susan had sprung from her chair and was at the door that led to the back of the house. She drew back in amazement. The door was unlocked!

"He must have come through here to let me in and forgot to lock it," she surmised, quietly opening the door.

Any moment Susan expected to see the hunched-over man, but as she stuck her head through the door there was no one in sight. Ahead of her was a hall, and beyond that another door. Susan hurried down the passageway, opened that door also, and cautiously stepped through. She was in the dining room in the rear wing of the house.

Susan knew she must act very quickly, or Bruce Webb would return to the living room before she did. Her eyes scanned the room, looking for anything that might provide a clue. A magnificent stone fireplace graced one wall, beautiful pieces of cherrywood furniture filled the room, and the prisms of the lovely crystal chandelier tinkled faintly.

Spotting two doors, Susan crept silently over to first one and then the other, gingerly opening them. She found only closets, empty except for a few old clothes.

Then something caught Susan's eye. Lying under the magnificent dining-room table was a small piece of twisted metal. The young girl picked up the object and examined it.

"This looks like a hook from a Christmas tree ornament," she thought, thrusting the find into her purse. "What is it doing here in May, and why is it so shiny and new-looking?"

All at once Susan was certain she had heard a muffled noise. Was Bruce Webb returning to the living room? No, the noise came from the other direction, somewhere beyond the room she was in. There it was again, and this time the sound was that of a human voice.

"Louis, please let me out," the voice seemed to be saying.

"Oh, that has to be Teresa," reasoned Susan. "Louis is probably the hunched-over man. But where is she hidden?"

Momentarily perplexed at what her next move should be, Susan stood frozen to the floor. Then she noticed a third door, way over toward one side of the room.

"That most likely leads to another room," she judged. "Or maybe even to the cellar. But I can't investigate it now. I have to get back to the living room."

There was the voice again, plaintively calling,

"Louis, please let me out!" but Susan rushed from the room, closed the door, and ran down the hall. Grasping the knob of the living-room door, she tried to pull it open, but the door would not budge.

"He's locked it!" she gasped in panic. "I'm trapped!"

## Chapter XVI

## *Fast Talking*

"I TOLD YOU to keep this door locked," said a man's voice from the other side of the door.

"I forgot to when that old lady showed up, Louis," replied Bruce Webb. "Where did she go?"

"What old lady?" asked the man called Louis. "You mean you let somebody into this house?"

While Susan Sand listened from the hall, she knew she had to decide immediately what to do. Louis must be the name of the hunched-over man. Soon he and Bruce Webb would be looking for her. If she was going to try to escape, she would have to find a rear door and then make her way around the house to the taxi. Then suddenly she changed her mind.

"No, I'll confront them. It will seem less suspicious," she thought, and she knocked on the door. Her heart was pounding wildly. She must play her part well!

"Who are you, and what are you doing in the hall?" Louis cried out as he opened the door. He was the hunched-over man.

"The rug, sir," replied Susan meekly. "I was waiting for Mr. Webb to find the uniforms when I began to get curious about all these valuable antiques. I wandered into the hall and have been studying this beautiful Persian rug. It's authentic, you know."

"Is it?" said Louis, scratching his head.

"Most certainly. I must check with the Historical Society and see if we can afford to add this rug to our collection," continued Susan, leaning on her cane as she admired the intricate design.

"And just why did you decide to come here now?" asked the hunched-over man, his hands on his hips and an agitated expression on his face.

"Well, I'll tell you," began Susan slowly, crossing the room and sitting in the same chair she had occupied before. "The Historical Society had a tour through this house several years ago. The gentleman who owned the house at that time wouldn't sell one thing, and before I could get back to ask the new owner, Mr. Webb, if he would, he had left town. When I heard just yesterday that Mr. Webb had returned to Hollowhearth, I was overjoyed."

Susan sensed that the man called Louis was softening somewhat in his attitude toward her.

"Oh, I see you found the uniforms," she said suddenly, pulling herself up with her cane and walking to a sofa where Bruce Webb had laid the clothes. "My, but they are in remarkably good condition. All the buttons are intact, and there is even a medal pinned to the front of this one. Mr. Webb, I just must have these for our exhibition."

"How much will you give me for them?" Bruce asked somewhat impatiently.

"Well, now that I've seen them again, I realize they are even more valuable than I thought, especially the one with the medal," replied Susan cautiously. "Now if you included the rug, it would bring the price to several thousand dollars—but I couldn't pay you right now. I'd have to check with Mr. Pringle first."

"Hey, what is this?" snapped Louis suspiciously as he advanced toward Susan. "What's your game?"

"Young man, I don't know what you mean," Susan replied quietly. "I'm simply saying that I can't purchase these articles without consulting Mr. Pringle, the president of the Thornewood Historical Society. I merely stopped in to see if they were worth as much as I had supposed."

Bruce Webb's penetrating eyes were studying the elderly woman intently. All at once Susan wished she were out of the house, extricated from the predicament in which she now found herself. Slowly starting for the door, the young girl extended her hand to Bruce Webb, who reluctantly shook it.

"I'll be back, Mr. Webb. I promise you that," she said firmly, a slight smile on her lips. "And sooner than you think."

The taxi was still waiting, and Susan descended the porch steps carefully and climbed into the automobile as quickly as she dared. Once in the car, she leaned back, breathing a great sigh of relief.

"My, that was close," she told herself. "I'm sure they are confused. I hope I managed to allay their suspicions. At least I have answered two of the questions. Teresa is a prisoner somewhere in the rear wing, and the hunched-over man is called Louis. But where are the Stardrop Earrings?"

Then Susan remembered the clue she had found under the dining-room table. Opening her purse, she pulled out the little shiny, twisted piece of metal and examined it carefully.

"I have the feeling this fits in somewhere," she mused. "But where?"

All at once Susan had another idea, one that might be a lead to the discovery of the diamonds.

"Driver, take me to Crescent City," she said, "to Barbara Lauder's jewelry store."

As the taxi sped on to the town of Crescent City, Susan felt that she was abandoning Teresa, whose plaintive cry echoed in her ears. Perhaps the time had come to call in the police. If only she could discover the hiding place of the diamonds first, for then the case against Bruce Webb would be foolproof.

Louis was a member of the Crow People. Maybe he and Bruce Webb were both trying to escape from the infamous Black Hood, Sidney Crowden. But why was Teresa being kept a prisoner? Had the woman learned something and then threatened to tell what she knew?

All the way to Crescent City, Susan tried to straighten out what she had learned and fit the information into the proper order. She wondered about Dr. Endicott and how much danger he might be in, especially if he had been followed from Caracas. Because of his inquiry at the police station, the Crow People probably thought that the little professor might have information that was vital to them. Did the

Black Hood know that Bruce Webb was alive and living in Hollowhearth House?

Susan was still deliberating exactly how to approach Barbara Lauder, when the taxi arrived in front of the jewelry store. This time the girl dismissed the driver after paying him, hoping she would have no difficulty in finding another cab.

As she entered the store and looked around for the owner, Susan felt relatively secure in her disguise. Her masquerade had stood the test well at Hollowhearth.

The small store was lined with glass cases, each displaying expensive pieces of jewelry. On the wall was a plaque from the Crescent City Chamber of Commerce, attesting to Barbara Lauder's standing in the community.

"She's nothing but a fake and a crook," thought Susan angrily. "She probably handles all her fraudulent dealings in that isolated cottage and still passes herself off as an upstanding citizen."

While these thoughts were passing through Susan's mind, Barbara Lauder entered the store from a back room.

"May I help you?" she said in a cordial tone.

"Yes, if you would be so kind," replied Susan. "I'm looking for a pair of earrings. A gift for my niece."

"Is there anything special that you have in mind?" Barbara Lauder asked.

"My niece is very partial to diamonds," replied Susan, carefully watching the woman's face. "Especially the kind that hang loose—you know, a drop earring."

Barbara Lauder reached into a case and took out several pairs of diamond pendant earrings. Susan pretended to study each pair, picking them up in her gloved hands and holding them to the light.

"These are very lovely indeed," she said presently, "but the diamonds are rather small. Have you any that are larger?"

"Larger?" Barbara Lauder looked surprised. "Diamonds bigger than these would be tremendously expensive. I'm afraid these are the largest I have."

"But you know where I can find larger ones, don't you?" Susan asked.

"Certainly. In New York City at Cartier, Tiffany, Van Cleef and—"

"No, I don't mean another store," said Susan, interrupting her. "You know where I can get what I want not far from here."

"What are you talking about?" asked Barbara Lauder, narrowing her eyes and gripping the glass case.

"You know what I'm talking about," continued Susan almost in a whisper. "I know where you can get rid of those Stardrop Earrings with no questions asked. You'd get much more money for them."

Susan hoped she wasn't going too far. She was taking a desperate chance that Barbara Lauder's greed would overcome her suspicion. The woman stared at Susan in shocked silence for several moments.

"How do you know about the Stardrops?" she asked, her voice trembling.

"Quite a few people know about them," replied

Susan. "I know someone who would give plenty for them, more money than you could get anywhere else."

"Who?" Barbara Lauder was almost shaking with excitement.

"If you meet me in—"

Susan was about to suggest a meeting place where Barbara Lauder could be trapped into giving herself away to the police, when she noticed a car pull up on the other side of the street. The car was Bruce Webb's yellow convertible. Two men got out and started across the street to the jewelry store.

## Chapter XVII

## *A Vital Message*

"I CANNOT BE SEEN!" thought Susan Sand as Bruce Webb and Louis came toward the jewelry store. "I must escape through the back, if only there is a rear exit!"

Barbara Lauder had seen the men also and seemed momentarily confused.

"Miss Lauder," said Susan abruptly, "I don't think we should be seen together. Our transaction is too delicate. I will call you later and arrange a meeting place."

Before Barbara Lauder knew what had happened, Susan had disappeared into the back of the store, out of view of the approaching men. The young girl was convinced that she had not been followed from Hollowhearth House. She had been very cautious about that and knew that the yellow convertible had not been tailing her taxi.

"They are coming here on business," she told herself as she spotted a rear door. "They must still be trying to get rid of the Stardrop diamonds."

Just as Susan was heading for the rear exit, the men entered the store. She was able to hear some of the conversation.

"I told you never to come here," said Barbara Lauder. "It's not safe."

"This is an emergency," replied Louis. "We have to get those diamonds off our hands fast."

"I told you, I'm working on it," replied the woman.

Susan dared not wait any longer to listen to their conversation. She had already heard enough to convince her that Barbara Lauder was tempted by Susan's fake offer of more money, for the woman was trying to delay disposing of the diamonds.

"If my plan works, they will soon be fighting among themselves," Susan reasoned as she hurried down an alley and into a side street. "That should give me some time to find the diamonds. They haven't got rid of them yet, so the earrings must still be in Hollowhearth House."

Almost forgetting her disguise, Susan walked rapidly down the side street, carrying her cane. No taxi was in sight. The girl dared not wait on the corner, for at any moment the yellow convertible might appear and her plans would be ruined. So far her disguise had been successful, but she did not want to press her luck.

Susan boarded a bus when no taxi came into view, not certain what route she was taking. Once on the vehicle, she felt safe from detection. For several miles she remained on the bus and soon found herself in Oak River, where she changed to another bus, and within an hour she had reached the Thornewood station. A short walk brought her home to her impatient, worried friends and an anxious Professor Sand. Also waiting for her was an unexpected visitor, Mrs. Manning.

After the first excited greetings were over, Susan wearily sank into a chair and started to describe her narrow escape. The group sat in stunned silence. Professor Sand and Mrs. Manning were too fascinated by Susan's disguise to say a word. Finally Randall Scott spoke.

"So Barbara Lauder actually thought you could get her more money for the diamonds," he said.

"Yes, I was a trifle shocked to find she would double-cross Bruce Webb and Louis if she had the chance," Susan replied. "If we hadn't been interrupted, I could have trapped her into bringing the Stardrops to a prearranged meeting place. With the police waiting to arrest her, she would have been caught red-handed."

"Then that means that she knows where the earrings are," offered Brian.

"She certainly does," responded Susan. "And it's obvious that the men are getting nervous, because they are very anxious to dispose of the diamonds soon. That means that we must act quickly."

"But what can we do?" asked Marge in a startled tone.

"My plan is to contact Barbara Lauder tonight and arrange the meeting," explained Susan. "She will have to get the diamonds from the hiding place in Hollowhearth House first. We will have the police waiting when she shows up."

"That's a daring scheme, Susan," warned Aunt Adele. "What if she can't get the Stardrops from where they are hidden without being caught?"

"Your aunt is right," agreed Mrs. Manning. "Those men are desperate and will stop at nothing to gain their ends. Barbara Lauder will be in danger also if they suspect she is trying to double-cross them."

"I suppose you are right, Mrs. Manning," replied Susan pensively. "But why did you come to see me? With all that's happened, I completely forgot to ask you that."

"Well, Susan, to begin with, as you know, I quit my job," replied the cook. "I must admit that I'm glad to get out of that house."

"That's a relief to me, too," Susan answered.

"But that isn't the main reason I'm here," Mrs. Manning continued, her voice becoming grave. "It's because of that poor woman that I'm here."

"You must mean Teresa." Susan was tense with expectation. "How could you have seen her? She is a prisoner."

"A prisoner!" cried Mrs. Manning. "I knew she was terrified. That explains this letter I have here." The cook handed Susan an envelope.

"You see, I found it in my pocketbook, stuffed into the side pocket. I didn't know it was there until just a little while ago. The poor thing—Teresa—must have put it in my bag Saturday morning when I went to Hollowhearth House to cook breakfast. She wanted to talk to me, but that dreadful Bruce Webb didn't give her the chance. My pocketbook was on the table in the hall. That's where she had a chance to stuff this letter into it. It sounds mighty strange to me. As soon as I found it, I brought it straight to you."

"You were absolutely right in doing so," replied Susan, unfolding the letter. "Oh, look! It's about the Stardrop Earrings!"

Everyone gathered around Susan and read the brief message that Teresa had written. It consisted of a single phrase: "Stardrops in the Sea of Light?"

"What does it mean?" cried Marge. "'Stardrops in the Sea of Light'? It doesn't make any sense."

"It must make sense. Teresa risked a great deal to get this message into Mrs. Manning's pocketbook." Susan adjusted her glasses and intently studied the phrase. "This has to tell us where the diamonds are. It just has to!"

While Susan studied the paper, no one spoke for fear of interrupting her thoughts. Mrs. Draper slipped into the kitchen to prepare an afternoon snack, and Randall Scott paced from one end of the living room to the other, now and then peering over Susan's shoulder to reread the phrase.

"Is it possible that there is a Sea of Light somewhere, and that the diamonds are hidden in it?" ventured Marge. "Maybe they aren't in Hollowhearth House after all."

"They have to be," Susan insisted. "What about that package I saw Saturday night when I followed Bruce Webb, Louis, and Teresa to Barbara Lauder's cottage? The diamonds must have been in that package."

"Yes, you're right, Sue," answered Randall Scott, running his fingers through his hair in exasperation.

"And just a few hours ago they were talking in the

jewelry store about how to dispose of the earrings." Susan was talking more to herself than to anyone else. "No, those earrings are in Hollowhearth House. Teresa doesn't know exactly where they are hidden."

"How can you be so sure she doesn't know?" asked Brian.

"Because if she did she would have written at least a broad hint in her message. She had the courage to write the note and then to risk being seen putting it into Mrs. Manning's purse. That can mean only one thing—the Sea of Light is a secret code of Bruce Webb's and Louis's. Teresa must have heard them say it to one another. They don't want her to know where the earrings are hidden."

Susan was abruptly interrupted by the ring of the telephone. As the girl picked up the receiver and heard the voice on the other end, her expression became one of fright.

"Susan, this is Giles Endicott," said the voice. "They're after me. Please help!"

Then there was a click and the receiver went dead.

## Chapter XVIII

### *Alone and Trapped*

"IT'S DR. ENDICOTT. Something has happened to him!" said Susan Sand tensely, the telephone receiver still in her hand.

"What!" cried Randall Scott. "I never should have left him alone. What did he say?"

"He said, 'They're after me. Please help!'" she replied. "He must mean the members of the Crow People. He thought they followed him from Venezuela. I think the time has come to call the police."

Quickly Susan dialed the police emergency number and as clearly as possible explained the situation. The sergeant assured her that he would send a patrol car immediately to Professor Scott's home.

"What are we going to do?" asked Brian. "We can't just sit here and wonder what is happening."

"We're not going to," responded Susan decisively. "You and Marge go to Professor Scott's house to make certain that the police understand the gravity of the situation. Professor Scott, you and I are going to Hollowhearth House."

"To Hollowhearth—Why?" Randall Scott asked in surprise.

"To do some investigating," Susan answered, as the four of them headed for the door.

"How do we know that Dr. Endicott called from Professor Scott's home? He may not be there now," reasoned Marge.

"That's why Professor Scott and I are going to Hollowhearth House," explained Susan.

"You mean you think Dr. Endicott may be there?" Brian asked.

"It is a possibility," she responded. "The Stardrop Earrings are the cause of everything. If Dr. Endicott is now a prisoner, they may bring him to Hollowhearth House in their search for the diamonds. The Black Hood's men probably think he knows more than he actually does."

Without wasting further time, Susan and Randall Scott headed for Hollowhearth Hill, while Marge and Brian started for Professor Scott's house. Professor Sand and Mrs. Manning protested violently. Still in her disguise, Susan presented the picture of a very agile and alert old lady.

"Susan, I hope we are doing the right thing," Randall Scott cautioned. "What will we do when we get there?"

"We're going to get into the house," she replied firmly. "If we are lucky, Bruce Webb and Louis may still be at Barbara Lauder's jewelry store."

"And what if they are not? It is just as likely that they have returned by now."

Susan did not answer, for she realized that Professor Scott might be correct. However, she felt that they must take the chance, for Dr. Endicott's sake.

"'Stardrops in the Sea of Light,'" the raven-haired girl murmured to herself during the drive to Hollowhearth House. "What does it mean? And what about the little piece of metal I found? Could that have some connection with all of this?"

Upon reaching Hollowhearth Hill, Susan parked her car in the same wooded area she had used before. Cautiously, she and Randall Scott crept along the private road that led to the house.

"Look, the garage is empty," she whispered. "They haven't returned yet. If we can get into the rear wing, perhaps we can find Teresa and release her."

"Let's go around the house and see if we can enter by the back door," Professor Scott suggested. "You know, Susan, if we are caught, we could be arrested for breaking and entering."

"We'll just have to take that chance," responded the girl. "Teresa and the Stardrop diamonds are both hidden in Hollowhearth House, and we are going to find them."

Quickly crossing the driveway to the protection of the hedges on the opposite side, Susan and Professor Scott made their way to the back of the old house. The late afternoon sun still shone brightly in the cloudless sky, but the shadows from the huge trees cast an umbrella of shade over the structure. Nothing seemed to be stirring except the wildlife in the woods.

The back entrance to the house was securely locked, and the curtains were drawn across the windows so that no view of the interior was possible.

"I'm afraid we will have to abandon the entire idea," said Randall Scott, "unless you know how to pick a lock."

"We must get into that house," Susan staunchly replied. "There is a way to do it without wasting time trying to break down a door."

Just then she spotted an old cellar entrance, almost totally covered by ivy.

"There," cried Susan triumphantly, pointing to the two wooden doors. "A basement entrance!"

In no time Susan and Randall Scott were pushing away the thick growth of ivy and tugging at the rotted wooden doors, which seemed to lead directly into the ground. A single iron ring attached to one of the doors suddenly gave way, and the two sides swung upward, revealing a stone stairway.

Susan pulled a flashlight from the pocket of her skirt, and the two started slowly down the steps, soon reaching a hard dirt floor. They were in a small dark room, entirely empty except for a few rickety barrels and crates. On the left was another staircase, this time of wood, which led from the cellar to a door at the top.

"I should have brought a flashlight too," whispered Professor Scott, following Susan up the wooden stairs. "It's like the middle of the night down here."

The door at the top of the steps was not completely closed. The panels were warped with age and the hinges so rusty from disuse that the door hung half open.

There was not a sound from anywhere in the house as Susan stepped through the opening into another small room. Ahead was another door. Crossing to it, the girl quietly turned the knob and found herself in the kitchen.

"The dining room has to be over there," she thought, crossing the kitchen. "I wonder where Teresa is? So far there seems to be no place for her to be concealed."

With a sharp intake of breath, Susan stealthily listened at the kitchen door. She thought she had heard a noise, but now the house seemed completely silent. Slowly turning the knob, she opened the door several feet and peered into the dining room.

"Come on, Professor Scott," she urged, stepping into the room. "The dining room is empty."

There was no answer to her summons. Susan whirled around in the middle of the large room, but Randall Scott was nowhere to be seen.

"Where did he go?" she thought in confusion. "He was right behind me on the stairs."

All at once there was a noise from the hall and the sound of a key in a lock.

"They've returned!" gasped Susan. "Oh, where is Professor Scott?"

Realizing that she would not have time to go back across the dining room to the kitchen, Susan looked frantically about for a place to hide. Seeing a pair of long velvet draperies that covered one of the large windows, she slipped quickly behind them. Just as she did so, the dining-room door opened and she could hear several people entering the room.

For a seemingly endless period of time, Susan was able to hear voices from the opposite side of the wide room, but she could not hear what was being said.

One of the voices was definitely that of a woman. Cautiously, Susan parted the thick draperies and peeked out. There stood Barbara Lauder, Bruce Webb, and the hunched-over man, Louis.

As Susan continued to watch the three conversing, her keen eye spotted something by one of the closets opposite from her hiding place. In the dust directly in front of the closet door were two long marks, as if something had been dragged across the floor.

"Teresa!" thought Susan. "They've put her in the closet since I was here earlier. Why didn't she call out?"

Slowly the little group started to move nearer to the middle of the room. The two men had begun to argue violently.

"If you hadn't double-crossed the Black Hood and stolen the Stardrop, none of this would have happened," said Louis angrily.

"You're a fine one to talk," retorted Bruce Webb, clenching and unclenching his fists. "You're just as anxious to get the money from the diamonds as I am. If you hadn't been blackmailing me, saying you would go to the Black Hood, you never would have found out where the other earring was."

"It's a lucky thing for you I didn't tell the Black Hood that you are still alive," Louis cried out. "If he found out that you had never been on *El Cometa,* you wouldn't be standing here now."

"What about you stealing the other earring from that professor?" yelled Bruce Webb in response. "We're both in this together up to our ears!"

Susan listened to the violent argument in silent

amazement. "They're both terrified of the Black Hood," she told herself. "Louis doesn't know that the Black Hood's men followed Dr. Endicott from Caracas and are in Thornewood. The Crow People may be close on Bruce Webb's trail and might soon learn that the diamonds are in Hollowhearth House!

"Everyone seems to be chasing everyone else," she thought. "The Black Hood's men are after Bruce Webb and the Stardrops, and so am I. We'll see who is going to win the race!"

All at once Barbara Lauder interrupted the feuding men. "Look, we can't get anywhere with you two fighting," she said. "It's my job to get rid of the diamonds. I know the right people who will buy them at a good price."

"If you hadn't wasted so much time with that old woman and those uniforms this afternoon, we might have gotten rid of the diamonds by now," Louis continued, unmindful of Barbara Lauder's words.

"Old woman? What old woman?" asked Barbara Lauder. Suddenly her calm exterior had vanished. She looked extremely upset.

"She was perfectly harmless," defended Bruce Webb. "There's plenty of money in these antiques. That woman was willing to pay a lot for them."

"The old woman—what did she look like?" Barbara Lauder impatiently asked. "Did she carry a cane and wear her hair in a braid on the back of her head?"

"Yes, but how do you know that?" queried Louis.

"Yeah, why do you care about some old lady who wants to buy Civil War uniforms?" asked Bruce Webb offhandedly.

"Because there is something fishy about her, that's why," the woman shouted. "She came to my store this afternoon and asked about the Stardrops!"

"What!" the two men cried. "Why didn't you tell us?"

"Because I didn't think I could trust you," responded Barbara Lauder in a deliberate lie.

While the argument continued, Susan remained silent behind the draperies, desperately planning her next move. If she were caught now, especially still in her disguise, there would be no escape.

"Where is Professor Scott?" she thought, starting to feel panicky. "He couldn't just disappear. Where did he go?"

As Susan plotted what to do, the three continued to shout at each other.

"We've got to find that old woman, and fast," said Bruce Webb, his voice shaking.

"If she really is an old woman," responded Barbara Lauder. "She's smarter than the three of us put together, whoever she is."

"Well, we're going to start looking for her right now," Louis announced. "She and Teresa know too much about the diamonds. We have to shut them up."

As Susan listened fearfully, she suddenly realized that she had mislaid the cane that was part of her disguise. She could feel the blood drain from her face when she saw that the cane was leaning against the dining-room wall, in full view of her three desperate enemies!

## Chapter XIX

# *Escape*

"MY CANE!" gasped Susan Sand to herself. "If they see it, they will know I'm in the house. I've got to get out of here! But how?"

Through the crack in the draperies Susan watched as the trio continued to argue. She knew that one glance toward the corner by any one of them would reveal the cane, and her situation would become even more desperate.

"And just how do you propose we locate that old woman?" Bruce Webb asked angrily. "We have no idea who she is or where she might live."

"Well, she's not from the Historical Society," retorted Louis in a scathing tone. "Somehow she knows about the Stardrop Earrings. We've got to find her!"

"Where do you suggest we look?" Barbara Lauder asked sarcastically. "You two certainly have made a mess of things. First Teresa finds out about the diamonds, and now this supposed old lady—"

"*We* made a mess of things!" interrupted Bruce

Webb in a loud voice. "What about you? I'm not so sure you weren't planning a double-cross. Why, you may even be in with that old woman!"

While the argument continued, Susan was studying her hiding place behind the draperies. The window directly in back of her was her only means of escape.

"They will certainly hear me if I open it," she thought. "But I don't know what other choice I have."

From her cramped position, Susan turned slightly and cautiously pressed her forehead against the window. The distance to the ground was not considerable. Once outside, she would have to make a dash for her car—but how could she leave without Professor Scott? Where could he have disappeared to so suddenly? And what about Teresa? Was she in that closet across the room?

Every second that Susan remained behind the curtains lessened her chance of escaping. Her cane was bound to be seen at any moment. Slowly she started to ease herself around so that she would be facing the window. The slightest movement of the curtains could give her away.

The long, full skirt she was wearing made it difficult for her to move without disturbing the draperies. If only she could slip out of the skirt! Then she would be able to climb through the window and run more easily.

As Susan began to fumble with the button on the waistband, the voices of the trio continued to debate loudly how they were going to find the old woman. Susan could not help chuckling to herself, even though she was in great danger.

"They have no idea how close they are to finding her," she thought ruefully.

Suddenly Susan realized that the voices were not so loud. The three of them were leaving the dining room! Cautiously she peered through the crack. The door to the hall was open, but the room was empty.

"What a break!" she thought, drawing in a breath. "Oh, if only I could get to that closet and free Teresa!"

Without hesitating a second longer, she hurried from her hiding place and tiptoed across the room. The closet door was locked, but the key was in the keyhole. Slowly she turned the key and silently opened the door. There was Teresa, lying on the floor, bound and gagged!

Susan put her finger to her lips, indicating that they must be quiet, and then quickly undid the gag. Teresa's expression was one of amazement as she stared at the old woman before her.

"I'm Susan Sand," Susan whispered in explanation, untying the ropes. "This is the disguise I've been wearing. We have no time to lose. We must make a run for my car. It's parked down the road. Follow me!"

"You—you are marvelous," Teresa stammered, rising weakly to her feet. "I called and called when they had me locked in the cellar, but no one heard me. But you could have escaped without trying to save me. Never before have I met anyone like you."

Unmindful of Teresa's praise, Susan hurried from the closet, pulling her companion by the arm. There were voices coming from the living room. Susan grabbed her cane from the corner and slipped through the dining-room door into the kitchen.

"We'll try to get through the cellar," she explained to Teresa. "I came with Professor Scott of Irongate University. Now he's disappeared!"

"Oh, they must have him," moaned Teresa. "The Black Hood's men must have captured him."

"The Black Hood's men! Are they here?"

"I have not seen them," said the woman, following Susan down the wooden stairs to the cellar. "But I know how they work. They are looking for the diamonds. If they are lurking about the house and saw your friend, they may have captured him."

"Then you think that the Black Hood's men have discovered Hollowhearth House?" Susan asked.

"They must know by now that Bruce stole the diamond," replied Teresa, her face pale with fear. "It is only a matter of time before they will find him."

"Teresa, where are the diamonds? What does 'Stardrops in the Sea of Light' mean?"

"I am not sure, but—"

Suddenly there were footsteps above them in the kitchen. Teresa's escape must have been discovered.

"Run, Teresa!" cried Susan. "We must get to my car!"

Susan pushed up the cellar doors and scrambled through the opening. "Head for the woods, over there," she called over her shoulder. "My car is on the other side of the road, in a clearing."

Susan pulled her long skirt up well above her ankles and ran across the lawn into the protection of the woods. Looking back, she saw that Teresa was only halfway across the green expanse. Emerging through the cellar doors was Louis, and he was gaining rapidly on the woman. Right behind him was Barbara Lauder.

"Susan, keep going," cried Teresa. "You have to get away!"

Momentarily Susan hesitated. She realized that Teresa would soon be overtaken and that her rescue would be in vain.

"Marge and Brian are with the police at Professor Scott's house," she told herself. "Certainly they will bring the police here. But perhaps the Black Hood's men will capture me, as they must have captured Professor Scott. I have to keep going. It's our only hope."

With a wave of her hand to Teresa, Susan dashed on through the woods. The underbrush was thick and strewn with dead branches and leaves. Her heavy skirt greatly impeded her progress.

As she looked back over her shoulder, she saw Louis and Barbara Lauder violently struggling with Teresa. He had her by one arm, but with the other arm she thrashed out at Barbara Lauder, knocking the woman off balance. Bruce Webb was nowhere in sight.

Susan dared not waste time watching the scene behind her. She doubted that Teresa would be able to escape from a man as strong as Louis. She must get to her car and head for the highway.

As she raced on through the woods, her mind was a maze of confusing thoughts. Randall Scott's strange disappearance deeply disturbed her. She could not imagine what had happened to him. He had been right behind her—and suddenly he was gone.

If the Crow People had indeed captured him, where had they gone and why did they not enter the house to search for the diamonds? Could his captors be somewhere in Hollowhearth House in a secret hiding place? Certainly, if the professor had been attacked, she would have heard something. But there had not been a sound to indicate what could have happened to him.

And what about Dr. Endicott? What was the meaning of his plea for help? Where was he calling from? Could both he and Professor Scott be captives of the Black Hood's men?

Breathless, Susan reached her car and leaned against the door. Glancing back, she saw Louis making his way through the thick underbrush. She fumbled for her keys, pulled them from her purse, jumped into the car, and thrust the ignition key into place.

"Stay exactly as you are," ordered a masculine voice from the back seat. "If you move a muscle, you will be sorry."

Susan sat frozen in terror. In the rear-view mirror she could see the face of Bruce Webb glaring at her. As he moved forward, his hand reached over the upholstery. He was clutching a black revolver.

## Chapter XX

## *Lost in the Fog*

"SO YOU'RE the old woman from the Historical Society," said Bruce Webb in a mocking tone. "Seems to me you run awfully fast for a little old lady. I wonder how you'd look without your wig."

With one sudden jerk of his left hand, Bruce Webb yanked the white wig from Susan Sand's head. Her long black hair fell to her shoulders. Laughing loudly, her captor tossed the wig onto the seat next to Susan and grabbed the cane, which was leaning against the dashboard.

"I'll just take this in case you have any ideas about banging me over the head," he declared. "I must say, you really had me fooled."

"Thank you for the compliment," Susan quietly replied. "You won't get away with it, you know. The police already know where you are."

"Oh, they do, do they," interrupted Louis as he approached the car from the woods. "If that's really true, we'll just have to make sure you are not here when they arrive."

"What do you suggest we do with her?" Bruce Webb asked his accomplice.

"The same thing we're going to do with Teresa. Get rid of both of them."

Susan shuddered involuntarily. Her mind was racing in an attempt to think of a means of escape. The two criminals apparently had no idea that the Black Hood was close on their trail. For the time being, she thought it best to keep that information to herself.

"If you attend to Teresa, I'll take care of this one before anyone finds out where she is," said Bruce Webb.

Susan smiled to herself. She felt like blurting out that many people knew about her venture to Hollowhearth House, but she wisely remained silent.

"How do we know who else might know that this kid came here?" Louis returned, as if in response to Susan's thoughts. "We'd better dispose of these two right now and clear out of here."

At these words, Susan realized she had to gain time for herself, in the hope that Marge and Brian would soon arrive with the police. Her eye lit on the Crow tattoo on Louis's arm.

"I see you are a member of the Crow People," she casually said.

"Wha—how the—how do you know what this means?" Louis blurted, looking at his forearm.

"You'd be surprised just how much I know about the Black Hood."

The man's face blanched several shades lighter. He opened the car door and looked Susan directly in the face. "Teresa told you," he cried out.

"No, it wasn't Teresa," returned Susan in a calm voice.

"Louis, don't listen to her," said Bruce Webb, fingering his revolver. "She's stalling for time."

"Yeah, maybe you're right," the man replied warily. "But how do I know she's not working for the Black Hood?"

Bruce Webb laughed loudly, which angered Louis even more. "Her! Working for the Black Hood! You're beginning to lose your marbles, Louis."

Louis slammed the door and backed away from the car. "You take care of her, and I'll take care of Teresa," he said coldly. "I'll bring Teresa in my car so we won't be around if the police show up."

"What about the diamonds?"

"We leave them where they are. Nobody will find them, and they won't be found on us. We'll meet at Barbara Lauder's place."

Without further conversation, the hunched-over man strode off up the road to Hollowhearth House.

"Okay, Miss Susan Sand. Start the motor and drive where I tell you."

Bruce Webb was so close to Susan she could feel his breath on her neck. She had no choice but to follow his orders. He was cleverer than she had thought and must have reasoned that the best way to capture her would be to find her car. He knew she could not get away without it.

"Turn left at the highway," was the command. "And don't try signaling to anybody."

As Susan made the turn, she glanced anxiously in her rear-view mirror, hoping to see some sign of a police car. The traffic was light and some cars were putting on their headlights, for it was getting dark. The visibility was poor because of a thick fog that was beginning to drift in from the sea.

"Poor Teresa," thought Susan. "Another few minutes, and we would have escaped. If only we had had a little more time!"

Susan drove as slowly as she dared, all the time trying to plan a move to throw her captor off guard. Driving was becoming more and more difficult as the fog became thicker.

"Perhaps this fog is a stroke of luck," she thought. "I can't go too fast. If only he hadn't taken that cane away from me."

Bruce Webb had ordered Susan to head west, the opposite direction from Thornewood. She knew that the area they were traveling toward was less populated. There were many turnoffs onto country roads. About ten miles down the highway, Bruce Webb instructed her to leave the main thoroughfare.

Once she had turned off onto a narrow, bumpy lane, Susan began to feel an overwhelming fear. While on the highway she had been comparatively safe, but now there were no other cars in sight. As the fog rolled across the road like billowy clouds, she did not see how they could drive on much longer. Even her glasses were covered with mist.

"Where is he taking me?" she thought, trying to keep her nerves under control. "What's the point of driving endlessly through the fog?"

While Susan continued on, she began to formulate a plan. Any moment she expected to be ordered to stop. If she was going to escape, she would have to do it soon.

Without hesitating, the young girl suddenly stepped hard on the accelerator, violently lurching the car forward, then immediately pressed with all her strength on the brake. Bruce Webb, who had been leaning over the front seat, was thrown off balance onto the floor. Next, Susan stepped on the accelerator again and turned the wheel quickly to the right, throwing her car onto the soft shoulder of the road. In another second she was out of the auto and into the protection of the fog.

Susan ran as she had never run in her life. With no idea of where she was heading, she continued on, unable to see more than a few feet ahead. Behind her there was the faint fall of footsteps on the soft earth.

She crossed a marshy clearing covered with wet grass. Now, ahead of her, a heavily wooded area suddenly seemed to spring up out of the mist. She ran on into the woods, the footsteps keeping steady pace behind.

"'Stardrops in the Sea of Light,'" she said to herself as she made her way among the trees. Saying the phrase over and over seemed to take her mind off her pursuer. "'Stardrops in the Sea of Light.' That's the answer to everything, the reason I'm in this predicament."

All at once Susan became aware that the rapid footfalls behind her had stopped. There was nothing but silence and the damp, drifting fog. For a brief moment the young girl stopped and listened. Where had he gone? Somehow the silence was more frightening, because she had no way of knowing where her pursuer was, without the footsteps to guide her. Then there was a sudden muffled cry, followed by a dull thud. Had he fallen? If so, why did he cry out first?

Without moving an inch, Susan listened intently for another sound. Several seconds later she heard footsteps again, but this time they were walking rather than running. They seemed to be going away from her, for the sound was becoming less distinct.

"Why would he abruptly end the chase?" she asked herself. "If I could hear his footsteps, he certainly could hear mine. Unless . . ."

Without further hesitation, Susan started back in the direction of the footsteps. She tried to remain far enough away to make flight possible and yet keep near enough to follow the sound. For a quarter of a mile the pursuit continued.

She emerged from the woods and was again crossing the marshy clearing, only this time she seemed to be going in another direction. Then, without warning, she thought she heard voices. Yes! The sound was unmistakably that of a number of voices coming from somewhere in front of her.

Creeping slowly on, Susan gave a little gasp of astonishment. She had come upon the gaping mouth of a cave. Within, she could definitely hear men talking.

As Susan drew closer, a shadowy figure passed in front of a glow that came from within the cave. The figure was that of a tall, powerfully built man, and he was carrying another man over his shoulder. Susan

could barely see the face of the unconscious man, but as he was carried into the cave she was certain that he was Bruce Webb!

## Chapter XXI

## *The Crow People*

"BRUCE WEBB must have been captured by the Crow People!" reasoned Susan Sand as she watched the two figures disappear inside the cave. "What other explanation could there be? We were followed from Hollowhearth House!"

Cautiously Susan crept closer to the mouth of the cave. As she neared the entrance, the voices from within became louder, and she was able to hear some of the conversation.

"Good work, Ben," one voice said in a commanding tone. "Webb was foolish to think he could ever slip through our net."

"He was with some girl, Sid," was the response. "She got away in the fog."

"Sid!" said Susan, sucking in her breath. "Sidney Crowden, the Black Hood! He must have come all the way from South America!"

Overcome by curiosity, Susan slowly peered around the stone edge of the cave and looked in. Directly in the center of the dirt floor was a huge fire, which cast an irregular, eerie glow throughout the cavern. Nine men were seated around the fire, all wearing black hoods. One man was obviously the Black Hood himself, for he sat somewhat apart from the others and was speaking to the man carrying Bruce Webb.

"A girl? What would Webb be doing with a girl?" asked the leader.

"I don't know," came the reply. "Unless she's the one who was with that professor when we captured him."

Susan clasped her hand over her mouth to stifle an involuntary cry. Professor Scott was a captive of the Crow People! He must be somewhere inside the cave, perhaps in one of the many dark recesses.

While the conversation continued, Susan cast her eyes about the interior. Yes, there, over to the left, she thought she saw a figure huddled on the floor. As she stared at the spot, her eyes began to adjust to the dimness. There were several figures on the ground, some leaning against the stone wall and some lying down. She thought she counted five in all.

Susan drew back from the mouth of the cave and braced herself against the rocks that formed the opening. She had to collect her thoughts before she could decide on her next move.

"They have Professor Scott," she told herself. "But who else is a prisoner? Probably Dr. Endicott. That would explain his telephone call for help. Yet there are three more figures. Who could they be?"

The answer to Susan's question was not long in

coming, for the Black Hood continued to speak to the Crow People as they sat around the fire.

"We have all of them except the girl," he announced sternly. "We do not know how much information she has. Perhaps Louis or the two women can help us. Teresa! Who is the girl, and what does she know about us and the Stardrops?"

The pieces of the puzzle were rapidly falling into place for Susan as she listened at the cave entrance. The Black Hood's men must have captured Louis, Barbara Lauder, and Teresa right after she and Bruce Webb left Hollowhearth House. No other explanation was plausible.

Using the cave as a hideout, the Crow People were seizing anyone who they thought had any knowledge of the Stardrop diamonds. Dr. Endicott had probably been a prisoner ever since he telephoned Susan. Now she was the only one who knew the truth and was in a position to do something about her discovery!

Teresa had refused to answer the Black Hood's question about Susan. Louis, however, cried out, "She knows everything about us. If you don't find her, she will go to the police and you will all land in jail. Just let me go, and I will help you search for her."

"No!" boomed the Black Hood. "My men will look for the girl. You are my prisoner. You and Bruce Webb have double-crossed me. You will never escape!"

"Your men will not find her in this fog," responded Teresa in a spirited voice.

"Nine of my men against one girl? They will find her!" was the Black Hood's fiery answer.

Again Susan was forced to flee, but in which direction should she go? Then a daring idea occurred to her.

"Why should I run?" she reasoned. "I might not be able to find my car in the fog. No, I will hide right here in the bushes. They will never think of searching for me so close to the cave."

Quickly Susan darted into a thick growth of rhododendrons about twenty feet from the cave entrance. Crouching down out of sight, she knew she would not be discovered unless one of the Crow People was keen enough to search nearby.

Emerging from the cavern, the nine men began to spread out in different directions. Each was still wearing a black hood and carrying a flashlight. Soon they had all disappeared into the fog.

"I was right!" Susan said jubilantly. "Now the Black Hood is alone in the cave with his prisoners. If only I could get to Professor Scott and the others and free them."

Thinking quickly, she picked up a rock and tossed it past the cave entrance. She waited for several seconds and then threw another stone in the same direction. A moment later the Black Hood appeared in the opening and stood looking about.

"Is that you, Ben?" he called.

For the first time Susan could get a fairly good look at Sidney Crowden, for he had pulled off his hood in an effort to see better in the fog. He was extremely tall and muscular, with thick black hair and large, powerful hands. His bearing was that of a man accustomed to being in command.

As he stood with his arms folded across his broad chest, he turned his head in the direction of the rhododendrons, and Susan could see his thin-lipped, firmly set mouth and dark, penetrating eyes.

"Who's there?" he called again, advancing farther from the cave.

This time Susan threw a stone as far as she could. The sound of the rock striking the ground brought Sidney Crowden a good distance away from the cave's mouth. In a flash she had risen from her hiding place and was running through the opening, over to where the prisoners were.

Spotting Randall Scott, she hurried to him and started to untie the ropes that held his hands. The Black Hood, momentarily stunned by the sight of a figure in the clothes of an old woman, yet running like a girl, seemed unable to move. Then, realizing what she was doing, he ran back into the cave, roughly gripped her shoulders, and threw her against the wall.

"You're too late," said Randall Scott, shaking the loose ropes from his wrists. "I knew my college boxing would come in handy some day."

With one punch Professor Scott sent the Black Hood sprawling to the floor, where he lay perfectly still, apparently unconscious.

"Susan, are you hurt?" Randall Scott asked.

"No, just a little shaken. He only threw me off balance. I'll untie Teresa while you free Dr. Endicott. We must find my car before the Crow People return."

Somewhat dazed from his unexpected release, Dr. Endicott was slow in getting to his feet. "You are a most amazing girl," he said weakly.

"We must hurry, Professor Endicott," urged Susan. "I'll explain everything later."

"What about us?" cried Louis.

"You can't leave us here!" Barbara Lauder pleaded.

"Yes, we can," replied Randall Scott, quickly tying Sidney Crowden's ankles and wrists. "The police will save you from the Black Hood, if that's any consolation to you."

"You are safe with the police, much safer than you would ever be with the Crow People," Teresa said scornfully.

"Follow me," Susan urged, leading the group from the cave. "My car is somewhere across the field in this direction. Stay together. If we meet any of the Crow People, we might have a chance of fighting them off."

The fog was as thick as before, but the little group was grateful for the protection it offered. Susan judged the distance to her car to be about a quarter of a mile.

The four of them trudged on in single file. The only sound they could hear was that of their own footsteps. Within ten minutes, Susan emitted a joyful cry when she spotted her car only a few feet away.

"Hurry up. Luck's been with us so far," she whispered.

They piled into the auto, and Susan started the motor. At that moment a deep voice pierced the fog.

"Hey, Ben! There's somebody over here," the voice called.

"Step on it, Sue," cried Professor Scott. "They've heard us!"

"I am," returned Susan with alarm. "We're not moving. The tire must be stuck in the mud!"

## Chapter XXII

## *The Sea of Light*

"STUCK IN THE MUD! We can't be!" said Randall Scott, springing out of the car.

"They will catch us all!" screamed Teresa. "We must run, or it will be too late!"

"No, Teresa. Stay in the car," urged Susan Sand, laying a restraining hand on the woman's arm. "We may still be able to get going."

Randall Scott returned to the car and climbed in. "I can hear them out there in the fog. There are at least two men nearby, maybe three," he said.

"What about the tire?" Susan asked anxiously.

"It's stuck in the mud, all right. I put a rock under the wheel for leverage."

Again Susan pressed on the accelerator, and the car began to move slowly forward. With one final lurch, the quartet felt the wheel spin out of the mud and grip the hard surface of the roadway.

As the auto gathered speed, the figure of a man suddenly appeared through the misty darkness, directly in front of Susan's headlights. He was waving his arms violently and shouting at them as the car sped toward him. His black hood and wild gesticulations seemed unreal in the wisps of fog that drifted by.

Susan quickly swung the car to the right to avoid hitting him and continued on toward the main highway.

"We'll get you yet!" he shouted as the car raced away. "The Crow People will seek revenge!"

"Whew, that was close!" exclaimed Professor Scott. "Susan, having you for a friend is, to say the least, exciting."

"But extremely rewarding," chimed in Dr. Endicott. "I never expected to have such firsthand information on Sidney Crowden and the Crow People. They captured me right after I made that phone call to your home, Miss Sand. I saw one of them climbing in the kitchen window at Randall's, and I had just enough time to dial your number before he grabbed me from behind."

"You acted very quickly, Dr. Endicott," Susan replied. "You alerted us to the fact that the Crow People were in Thornewood. Now we must find Marge and Brian and the police. The Crow People cannot be allowed to go unpunished."

"Nor Bruce and Miss Lauder," added Teresa. "They were so greedy to have the Stardrop diamonds, they could not even trust each other."

"Teresa, you don't know where the diamonds are, do you?" asked Susan.

"In the Sea of Light, as I told you in my note."

"Yes, but what is the Sea of Light?"

"Ah, that I cannot tell you," replied Teresa regretfully. "I only heard Barbara Lauder and Louis talking about the Stardrops being in the Sea of Light. They thought I knew what that meant, but I do not. That is when they took me prisoner. They were afraid I would go to the police."

"Then we're right back where we started from," groaned Randall Scott. "The Sea of Light is probably a code name for the hiding place."

"We do have several clues," said Susan optimistically. "I think by piecing them together we will be led to the diamonds."

"What clues do you mean?" Teresa asked.

"First there is the Sea of Light itself," began Susan. "'Stardrops in the Sea of Light.' That is where the diamonds are actually hidden. We must decipher what it means."

"But we've tried," Professor Scott reminded her. "We didn't get anywhere."

"Yes, but there are other clues," Susan continued. "The twisted piece of metal, for instance."

"What twisted piece of metal?" Randall Scott asked in surprise.

"This," said Susan, pulling the shiny little hook from her purse. "I found it on the floor under the dining-room table in Hollowhearth House."

"But what significance could a tiny piece of wire have?" asked Professor Endicott in a mystified tone.

"It looks like a hook from a Christmas tree ornament," offered Professor Scott. "I don't see how you can attach any importance to it, Sue."

"This is the month of May—and this metal is new

and shiny. No one has lived in that house for five years. That hook was dropped on the floor recently," said Susan.

Then she was silent for some time, her brow knitted and an intense expression on her face. As the car flew along the highway, the other three occupants waited for her to speak further.

"Somehow I connect the little hook with that odd statement of Mr. Leeds'," she said thoughtfully. "The day I first went back to Hollowhearth House, I had a conversation with him. He told me that he saw Bruce Webb in the rear wing, reaching into the air. When Webb realized he had been seen, he rushed over and pulled down the shades."

"How strange!" said Teresa. "But what connection is there with the piece of metal?"

"I'm not certain yet," mused Susan. "But it all centers around the rear wing—the Sea of Light, the metal hook, and Bruce Webb's strange actions."

"Perhaps you're right," Randall Scott replied. "We know that the diamonds must be inside Hollowhearth House."

"And that's where we are going right now," Susan said determinedly. "To Hollowhearth House to find the hiding place."

"What about the police?" asked Teresa. "We should notify them right away, so that the Crow People and their prisoners do not escape."

"I'm hoping that Marge and Brian are already there with the police," Susan explained. "When they didn't find Dr. Endicott at Professor Scott's house, the next place to look would be Hollowhearth House. They knew that's where Professor Scott and I were going."

"And if they are not there, then what?" asked Dr. Endicott.

"We'll telephone headquarters and then search for the diamonds ourselves," Susan responded.

"But what if the Black Hood should be released from his bonds and return to Hollowhearth House with his men?" cried Teresa, her eyes wide with fear. "We would be his prisoners again. And there are so many more of them than we had expected."

"Teresa, we must take the chance," Susan soothingly replied. "If we don't find the Stardrops soon, we may never get another opportunity."

"Susan is right," said Randall Scott. "Bruce Webb will be forced to tell the Black Hood where he hid the diamonds before long. Right now, we are only a step ahead of the Crow People."

The fog continued as heavy as before, but in a relatively short time Susan reached the turnoff that led to Hollowhearth Hill. Instead of parking in the clearing, she drove on up the hill and parked in the driveway of the house.

Hollowhearth House looked completely deserted. There was a single light on the porch, and the front door was half open, but an ominous stillness had settled on the old structure.

"I can't imagine where Marge and Brian are," said Susan, mounting the porch steps. "At least we won't have to break in through the cellar. Someone has left the door open."

"The Black Hood's men probably forgot to close it when they captured Barbara Lauder and Louis," surmised Professor Scott. "When they caught me on the cellar stairs, they moved so swiftly and silently I didn't know what had happened."

The four of them entered the house and crossed the large living room to the rear wing. Susan switched on the light and stood looking around the dining room, where only a short time before she had had such a narrow escape.

"The Stardrop Earrings are somewhere in this room," Susan said emphatically. "Somewhere in the Sea of Light."

Minutes went by while she stood and studied the huge room. Her three companions waited patiently, somehow expecting her to discover the diamonds as if by magic. They were not disappointed.

With a sudden burst of enthusiasm Susan grabbed one of the dining-room chairs and pushed it toward a spot in the center of the floor, directly under the magnificent crystal chandelier.

"The Sea of Light," she cried out, pointing to the chandelier. "The Stardrop Earrings are hanging among the crystal pendants of this chandelier!"

While her audience watched in stunned silence, Susan climbed daintily onto the oval cherry table, which was directly under the chandelier, and reached her fingers among the prisms.

"They're here, I know they're here," she kept repeating, almost to herself. "They have to be here—yes, they are hanging from hooks just like the one I found under the table. My goodness, they are beautiful!"

"Oh, Susan," cried Teresa, climbing onto the table.

"You found them! You found the Stardrop Earrings!"

"Here, I've loosened the hooks," said Susan, carefully pulling her hand from among the crystal pendants. "See how they look as a pair!"

Dangling from Susan's hand were the two pear-shaped diamond earrings. The magnificent gems sparkled brilliantly, swinging from the hooks that had suspended them from the chandelier.

"Bruce Webb was hanging the diamond he stole when Michael Leeds saw him through the window," said Susan, gazing at the stones as they caught the light and reflected the colors of the rainbow. "He saw Bruce Webb reaching into the air to hang the earring in the chandelier."

"Of course, Sue!" cried Randall Scott as he stared at the gems in disbelief. "He was afraid Leeds would see what he was doing."

"And the Crow People were lurking about the house, hoping to discover where he had hidden them," reasoned Teresa.

"Yes, only they had to resort to taking everyone prisoner," said Dr. Endicott. "Apparently only Susan Sand could figure out the meaning of the 'Sea of Light.'"

All at once the group stopped talking and looked toward the front of the house. The sound of a car driving up, followed by the slamming of doors, had alerted them. A moment later, footsteps sounded on the porch.

"Oh!" gasped Teresa as the footsteps came closer. "I hope it is the police, and not the Black Hood and his men!"

## Chapter XXIII

## *An Interrupted Party*

"MARGE!" cried Susan Sand as her redheaded friend stepped into the dining room from the hall, followed by Brian, Chief of Police Burton, and several officers.

"Susan, we couldn't imagine what had happened to you!" exclaimed Marge. "We were here an hour ago, and there was no sign of you or Professor Scott."

As briefly as possible, Susan explained about her escape from Bruce Webb and her discovery of the Black Hood's cave.

"And you found the diamonds!" Brian cried in surprise.

"Susan found them," Teresa declared. "We just gave her moral support. They were hanging in the chandelier—in the Sea of Light."

"The chandelier is the Sea of Light! Of course!" Marge exclaimed. "How simple the explanation is, once you know what it means."

Susan smiled happily at Marge and then turned quickly to the police chief.

"Chief Burton, you must start for the cave right away," she said. "You may already be too late to round them all up."

As briefly as possible, Susan gave him directions on how to reach the cave by telling him where to turn off the highway, the country roads which she had taken, and then the approximate spot where she had parked her car.

"The cave is about one-quarter mile east through the woods. I hope you will notice the deep ruts my tires must have made in the mud," she added.

"The fog is lifting," Chief Burton said, turning to the door. "I'll call for plenty of reinforcements over my car radio. They won't get far away from this area." He and his men rushed away.

"There is an awful lot about this I still don't understand," said Marge in a perplexed tone. "When Brian and I got to Professor Scott's home, Dr. Endicott wasn't there, so we came here to Hollowhearth House. We were so worried when we didn't find you—we were sure something terrible had happened. Then we went back to the professor's house."

"Chief Burton was about to start a search of the entire vicinity when he decided to come back to Hollowhearth House on the chance that you would be here," Brian explained. "In the meantime, you have the whole case solved and even found the earrings. It looks as if we missed all the fun."

"There are still some points to be cleared up," replied Susan, carefully placing the Stardrop Earrings on the dining-room table. "Bruce Webb has a lot of explaining to do about Venezuela and how he got away with the one diamond."

"I can tell you about Venezuela," said Teresa, sinking into a nearby chair. "Bruce is my husband. I am the adopted daughter of Sidney Crowden and have known no other father but the Black Hood. All my life I suspected how terrible my stepfather was, but he treated me well and I had no reason to complain.

"I knew of the Stardrop Earring my entire life. Several times it was shown to me and I was told of the existence of another earring just like it that had been left behind in America two hundred years ago. I knew that the Crowdens remained loyal to the King of England and had to flee from the American Revolutionaries.

"Five years ago I came to Thornewood with Sidney Crowden and his nephew, Louis. I suspected that they were looking for the Stardrop Earring that their ancestor had left behind in his haste, but I had no way of knowing the truth, for they told me nothing. That is when I met Bruce Webb and fell in love with him."

"You were in love with Bruce Webb?" Marge asked incredulously.

"I know it sounds strange now, but at the time I thought he loved me. I did not know that he wanted to gain information from me about the diamond."

"So he was using you," Susan responded sympathetically.

"But how did he find out the Stardrops even existed?" asked Randall Scott.

"I innocently told him of the one earring that the

Black Hood had in Caracas and of the existence of its mate in America. He must have surmised why Sidney Crowden and his nephew had come to Thornewood."

"But they didn't find the other earring," Brian stated. "How did they know it was in Piper Hall?"

"They knew that Piper Hall was the home of the Crowdens before the Piper family owned it, and that Nathaniel Crowden must have had a hiding place somewhere in that building. I knew they hadn't found it because they were so angry at the end of our stay in Thornewood. When we returned to Venezuela, Bruce Webb came back with us, and a year ago we were married."

"When did you decide to escape to the United States?" asked Brian.

"After the Stardrop was stolen and my husband was supposed to have drowned on *El Cometa*," Teresa responded, placing her hands over her face to stifle a sob. "I became terrified of the Black Hood and of Louis Crowden. I thought that they thought I was involved in the theft."

"Did you know that Bruce Webb had not drowned on *El Cometa*?" Randall Scott asked her after Teresa had composed herself.

"Yes, I always knew the truth," the pretty, dark woman slowly answered. "But I never told the Black Hood. My husband boarded *El Cometa*—he had booked passage—and then he slipped off the ship in order to fool the Crowdens.

"He knew they were after him, so he hid outside Caracas, and as soon as he heard the ship had sunk and that everyone on board was drowned, he took a plane to New York. He realized that the Crowdens would think he was dead. Right before he left, he came to me secretly one night and begged me to go with him.

"I was so overcome at seeing that he was still alive, I almost accompanied him, but I wanted no part of the theft. Then, after he left and I began thinking about him, I decided I would follow him on the next plane and beg him to return the diamond."

"Now all the pieces of the puzzle seem to fit into place," Susan stated triumphantly. "Louis Crowden followed Bruce Webb to America. He suspected Bruce had brought the diamond to Thornewood, and somehow Louis must have heard that Marge had inherited the house. He thought Marge might lead him to Bruce Webb, and he was afraid that if she managed to obtain the title to Hollowhearth House, he would have to break into her home to look for the diamond. He had to spy on her to try to find out what was going on."

"Louis Crowden was not positive that my husband was alive," Teresa said. "But when I suddenly disappeared, he suspected that Bruce had escaped to the United States and that I had followed him. Only after he got to America did he manage to definitely discover that Bruce had not drowned and was living in Hollowhearth House."

"And that's when Louis decided on blackmail," offered Dr. Endicott. "Louis Crowden realized that Webb wanted the Black Hood to think he was dead. He had an excellent weapon."

"And the Crow People followed you back to the United States, Dr. Endicott, because they thought you knew much more than you actually did," said Randall Scott.

"But, Teresa, weren't you afraid to follow Bruce Webb? You knew he was a thief," Susan asked gently.

"I was frightened, Susan," Teresa answered, almost in a whisper. "But I no longer wanted to live with the Crow People. Believe it or not, I felt safer with Bruce than I ever did with the terrible Crowdens. I thought I might be able to get my husband to return the earring.

"When Louis Crowden came to Hollowhearth House and I went to the door and saw him standing there, I fainted. I thought he was going to take me back to Venezuela."

"But instead he was so greedy that after he had stolen the other diamond from Professor Scott, he went in with Bruce Webb, because as a pair those earrings are worth a fortune," Susan stated in disgust.

"What will become of the Stardrops?" asked Marge. "Who will own them?"

"I would imagine that the earring Susan found in Piper Hall will belong to Irongate University," replied Randall Scott. "The other one still belongs to Sidney Crowden."

"What! Even though he's a crook?" Marge cried indignantly.

"It's belonged to the Crowdens for two centuries," said Susan. "The original theft occurred too long ago for anyone else to claim ownership."

While the discussion continued, Susan called her home and quickly explained the events of the afternoon to her aunt. Professor Sand insisted that Susan bring everyone home to dinner. Mrs. Draper had a large roast in the oven and plenty of food in the freezer, and would be delighted to have them all over to enjoy a good meal.

"Where will we put the earrings?" asked Brian as the little group left Hollowhearth House. "The banks are closed by now."

"We have a wall safe in the study," Susan replied, placing the earrings in her purse. "They'll have to stay there until tomorrow. I hope Chief Burton and his men have rounded up the Crow People. We don't want the earrings stolen again!"

Everyone laughed heartily as Randall Scott and Dr. Endicott climbed into Susan's car and Teresa and Brian into Marge's, and the two automobiles started for Thornewood.

Upon arriving at the big stone house where Susan lived, they were all delighted to find that Mrs. Manning and Michael Leeds had also been invited to join the festivities. Mrs. Manning had brought a luscious chocolate cream pie she had made that afternoon, and Mr. Leeds an exquisite bouquet of flowers from his garden to use as a centerpiece on the dining-room table.

Before Susan placed the Stardrop Earrings in the wall safe, the little group gazed in wonder at the huge, sparkling jewels.

" 'Stardrops in the Sea of Light,' " said Marge. "And it was Susan who figured out that the Sea of Light was the crystal chandelier."

"To think that they've been separated for two hundred years and are finally back together," sighed Mrs. Draper.

"It's a shame that one of them will still belong to the Black Hood," Teresa said angrily. "They should never be separated again. What good will it do Sidney Crowden if he is in jail?"

"These gems have caused a great deal of trouble," Professor Sand commented thoughtfully. "I'll be relieved when they are safely in the bank."

Before dinner, Susan went to her room to remove her disguise and change into proper clothes for the dinner party. By the time she returned to the dining room, the meal was ready and all the guests were seated around the large table.

Long after the chocolate cream pie had been enjoyed, they were still sitting at the table, sipping coffee and talking animatedly. Shortly after nine o'clock the front door chimes sounded, and Mrs. Draper went to answer them. To the amazement of the entire group, Chief Burton entered the room, accompanied by Bruce Webb.

"We rounded up all the Crow People and Barbara Lauder," he announced to his stunned audience. "Mr. Webb insisted that I bring him over. He has something he wants to say."

For several moments Teresa's husband stood uncomfortably before the dining table, his eyes wandering restlessly from one person to the other. Finally his gaze settled on Marge.

"I came to say I'm sorry about Hollowhearth

House, Marge, and I—I want you to have it," he stammered. "I'll sign it over to you and make it legal. It should have been yours all along."

Without another word, Bruce Webb walked over to Teresa, whispered something in her ear, and kissed her on the cheek. Then, nodding self-consciously to the others, he left the room with Chief Burton. Before the shocked dinner party could recover from the astounding announcement, the police chief turned back into the room.

"I completely forgot about the diamonds," he said with a sheepish grin on his face. "Sidney Crowden has some crazy idea about something called the Crowden Curse. He thinks that he and his Crow People were caught because of the earrings. He says he never again wants to see the diamond that belongs to him and that he'll sign a statement giving his earring to Irongate University."

"The Crowden Curse!" cried Teresa. "I always knew the Black Hood was superstitious. He used to talk about a curse being on the Crow People, and he wondered what caused it. How lucky you are that he decided it was the earrings!"

"I can't believe it!" shouted Marge. "Hollowhearth House is mine, and the Stardrops belong to Irongate!"

"I am so happy," said Teresa, with tears in her eyes. "Bruce will serve his time in prison and then come back to me. This experience has changed him. He will never get into trouble again."

"Now every time I go up the stairs to my office and see that stained-glass window, I'll think of the hood who once lived in that house," said Randall Scott, smiling boyishly. "Maybe we should rename the building Crowden Hall."

The party laughed uproariously at the young man's wit. Then, after champagne had been passed around, and Ikhnaton had joined the group, everyone turned to Susan and raised glasses in a toast.

"To the young lady who solved the mystery at Hollowhearth House," said Dr. Endicott, his eyes twinkling. "Mysteries seem to seek you out, my dear."

The little professor's words would prove to be prophetic, for events would shortly plunge Susan Sand into *The Secret of Clovercrest Castle.* For the moment, however, the famous author-sleuth smiled warmly at her friends, happy in the thought that her first case had come to such a successful conclusion.